T0279249

ENOLA HOLMES

AND THE MARK OF THE MONGOOSE

Also by Nancy Springer

THE ENOLA HOLMES MYSTERIES

The Case of the Missing Marquess

The Case of the Left-Handed Lady

The Case of the Bizarre Bouquets

The Case of the Peculiar Pink Fan

The Case of the Cryptic Crinoline

The Case of the Disappearing Duchess

Enola Holmes and the Black Barouche

Enola Holmes and the Elegant Escapade

ENOLA HOLMES

AND THE MARK OF THE MONGOOSE

Nancy Springer

WEDNESDAY BOOKS
NEW YORK

First published in the United States by Wednesday Books, an imprint of St. Martin's Publishing Group

ENOLA HOLMES AND THE MARK OF THE MONGOOSE. Copyright © 2023 by Nancy Springer. All rights reserved. Printed in the United States of America. For information, address St. Martin's Publishing Group, 120 Broadway, New York, NY 10271.

www.wednesdaybooks.com

Designed by Omar Chapa

The Library of Congress has cataloged the hardcover edition as follows:

ISBN 978-1-250-88573-9 (hardcover)
ISBN 978-1-250-88574-6 (ebook)

Our books may be purchased in bulk for promotional, educational, or business use. Please contact your local bookseller or the Macmillan Corporate and Premium Sales Department at 1-800-221-7945, extension 5442, or by email at MacmillanSpecialMarkets@macmillan.com.

First Edition: 2023

10 9 8 7 6 5 4 3 2 1

To all the writers who inspired me.

ENOLA HOLMES

AND THE MARK OF THE MONGOOSE

Prologue

"He has taken to calling me 'Cotswold,'" remarked Wolcott Balestier, smiling at his sister as they took tea together in front of the hearth.

"Then he is fond of you." Caroline Balestier smiled back not quite as sweetly—her brother had a more gentle, affectionate temperament than she did. Here they were, two Americans in London, England, because his foolish, idealistic notions had taken him hither, and it therefore followed that she, forsooth, had to go, too. It was an undisputed fact in society's mind that every gentleman needed a woman—mother, sister, wife, it didn't matter—to "do for" him.

"Carrie? What is it?" his kind voice asked, and she realised she must have been glowering.

"Oh, nothing. Nothing at all." Mentally shaking herself, she smiled and took a scone. "Is your business with him going well?"

"Almost better than I can believe. He has invited me to write a novel together with him, and he never does that! He writes rings around everybody. He writes rings around me!" So serious he forgot to eat, Wolcott leaned towards her. "He is really, truly a genius with words, Carrie. In my ten years in publishing, I've never met, or expected to meet, a man with a more outstanding literary gift."

"What makes him so outstanding?" asked Carrie, speaking quite lightly so as to conceal her own deep feelings. She had met the man a few times, but once would have been enough. A vital, muscular man, he was so much the opposite of her gentle, slender brother that the two of them formed a most unlikely alliance, and Carrie marveled to think of Wolcott's friend: his blunt, magnetic intensity, his brilliant talk about his many adventures, his enthusiasms and sometimes his despairs—it was rumored that he had suffered a nervous breakdown not long ago! His tempers—this was a man who truly needed a strong woman to do for him! She had already made up her mind to marry him.

Wolcott, stirring his tea thoughtfully, had not yet answered her. "Cotswold?" she addressed him playfully.

He looked up at her with a gaze far older than would seem possible for a young man in his twenties. "It's his passions, or rather, his convictions," said Wolcott. "Many people can write, but few have such force of soul. Here, Carrie." He started exploring his waistcoat pockets with slender fingers. "I looked over his shoulder as he was penning this, and it impressed me so much that I copied it. Here." He handed her a much-folded sheet of paper. "Read that."

She read. It started in mid sentence: ". . . the austere love that springs up between men who have tugged at the same oar together, and are yoked by the intimacies of toil. This is a good love, and, since it allows, and even encourages, strife, recrimination, and brutal sincerity, it does not die, but grows, and is proof against any absence. . . ."

As opposed to the not-so-austere love between a man and a woman?

Thinking this, Carrie looked up with a bleak feeling, but she was not going to let it conquer her; all things were possible and could be dealt with. She said quite evenly, "I have never heard of such a thing."

Wolcott gave her a small, skewed smile. "You and most people, I imagine. But Ruddy is different."

Again completely controlling the timbre of her voice, Carrie asked, "Is that what you think he looks for from you? 'The austere love of men who have toiled together?' Is that why he is asking you to co-author a novel with him?"

"It might be," said Wolcott.

Chapter the First

The front door opened so suddenly and forcefully that it badly startled me, causing me to pencil a ruinous scrawl across the conic sections I was so carefully drawing for my geometry class. Vexed, I looked up to see Joddy, the boy-in-buttons, hurrying to offer his tray to take the visitor's card, but the man brushed past him to stride towards my desk, causing an odd pleating effect within my mind, as if time folded and compressed. After all, it had been less than a year since I had made peace with my much older brothers, Sherlock and Mycroft Holmes, while before that I had been on the run from them, terrified of them, and in disguise. Therefore, even though I was now free to be my youthful self in a tailored linen suit with skirt cut short just below my ankles—even though I was now at liberty to be the real-life, very modern, May 1890 Enola Holmes—it's small wonder that once again I felt myself to be the fussy-frilly and obedient Ivy Meshle at her job in the reception vestibule of the great Dr. Ragostin's office. After all, the sign was still painted on the front window: *Dr. Leslie Ragostin, Scientific Perditorian.* (An impressive way of saying that the completely imaginary doctor, my "cover," purported to be a finder of missing persons.)

"Where's Ragostin?" barked my visitor, addressing me principally with his cleft chin, above which I saw mostly a great deal of dark brown moustache, bristling eyebrows, and thick spectacles. He could not have been more than twenty-five years old, dressed like a gentleman but quite lacking a gentleman's manners.

He looked familiar, distantly, as if he might be a Somebody I had seen in the newspaper, and he was handsome in a forceful way . . . for whatever reason, he put me sufficiently off balance so that I found myself uttering a meek Meshle sort of reply. "Dr. Ragostin is not here, but I am authorised to help you. Please be seated."

He did no such thing, but continued to tower over me, his moustache hiding everything about his mouth but the very middle of his lower lip; I wondered how he circumnavigated that biscuit-duster in order to eat. He was saying, loudly, "I need Ragostin to find Wolcott Balestier!"

Pencil in hand, I tried to write it down. "Would you spell—"

"He may be a victim of foul play! I've alerted Scotland Yard, but they won't listen to me!"

I tried again. "Would you please—"

"It's those vermin venomous pirates have got him!"

I verily felt my eyes widen at that. "Pirates?" A black flag bearing a skull-and-crossbones fluttered in the wind of my mind.

"Craven back-stabbing cowards! They'd better not hurt my chum Cotswold!"

"Who?" I demanded, meaning the most intriguing pirates, seafaring marauders with sneers picturesquely scarred by the sword.

"My mate! My buddy! The best friend a man ever had! Wolcott Balestier!"

Oh, bother. We were back where we started. "Would you *please* spell the name, please?"

At last, and quite loudly, he did so. I copied it on top of my spoilt conic sections.

"Where's Ragostin?" he insisted. "I'm told he's the specialist!"

"I am authorised to handle the preliminaries," I soothed. Actually, "Dr. Ragostin," who was entirely a figment of my imagination, had gone out of business in July of the previous year, when I had ceased to need him to protect me from the way Mycroft and Sherlock insisted on interfering with my life. Now on amicable terms with them, I was pursuing my education and had almost concluded my first year in the Women's Academy. So, faced with my loud and vehement visitor, I should have left Dr. Ragostin in retirement, but there was something about the idea of pirates—might the missing victim have been forced to walk the plank? I was quite fascinated. "What is Mr. Balestier's relationship to you?"

"Friend!"

"And his home address?"

He answered me only partially. "Maiden Lane! Where's Dr. Ragostin, the damn quack?" Such was the crude urgency with which this man spoke, nearly shouting. "He must find Cotswold!"

Cotswold was the name of a region in England near the River Severn, but evidently this pepper-pot of a man meant it as the nickname of a person, for, thrusting his tobacco-stained hand into his waistcoat, from some hidden pocket over his heart he drew a small photograph of the face of a man no older than himself, but in many ways quite his opposite. "Cotswold" had no bristling visage, no scrub-brush moustache, and no eyeglasses. Indeed, he had skin as fine as a lady's, gentle arched brows over large, intelligent eyes, an elegant nose, and a wide but subtle mouth ever so slightly smiling. Reaching for the photograph, I noticed Cotswold's immaculate collar, tidy hair, puckish ears, modest yet sufficient chin. But my vehement visitor did not yield the photograph; he snatched it away from me and slipped it back into his waistcoat.

"I want Ragostin!" he demanded again.

I answered quellingly, "I will tell him—"

"I will damn well tell him myself!" Lunging past my

desk to the double doors of the office proper, the impetuous young man first pounded on them, then tried to thrust them open, only to find they were locked.

Necessarily, in order to turn around and see whether he would next try to break his way in, I stood up. "There's only an empty room in there," I told him, still patient because, willy-nilly, although I had thought I was on hiatus from my life's calling of locating missing persons and things, I had become interested in the case. "Now, if you will give me your name—"

"I'll do no such thing!" Fists clenched, he wheeled to glare at me. "I'll deal directly with the professional or not at all!"

That struck a nerve, and so much for patience. I glared straight back at him, and because I am tall, our dueling stares quite equally clashed at close distance, intensified by the thickness of his spectacles. With fervor I told him, "I *am* the professional! Dr. Leslie Totally Fictitious Ragostin is merely my most unfairly necessary pseudo-masculine identity. I myself am the scientific perditorian, the finder of the lost! I—"

I was going to vow to find his friend, but he cut me off with a most appalling curse. "You?" he went on, wild-eyed and yelling. "You ostrich biddy with the mouth of a muleteer! You mud-head snipe-nose, you are the she-demon Putana who sucks men's blood, whose milk poisons babies! Banish yourself! Aroynt thee!"

I admit I stood there open-mouthed, speechless, yet someone spoke for me. A child's valiant voice shrilled, "Look 'ere, yer don't talk to Miss 'Olmes that way!" Joddy shoved his small self between me and the raving visitor.

Who seized him by the ear as if to lift him off the floor by that frail appendage.

Joddy yelled out in pain.

Whipping my dagger out of my bosom, I addressed its point to the disagreeable man's throat and told him, "Let the boy go."

Open-mouthed and speechless in his turn, he did so. But then his jaws clamped shut and his arm shot out, his hard hand grabbing for my wrist to disarm me.

I dodged him, dagger still at the ready, and as for Joddy, he grabbed the police whistle from my desk and ran to the front door, flinging it open to blow a shrill summons.

Coolly I informed the visitor, "According to the

Children's Charter that Parliament passed last year, it is no longer legal in England to harm innocents."

"Fatuous girl, put your pig-sticker down before you hurt yourself!"

Instead, I took a step back, tossed the dagger upwards, then caught it neatly by the hilt with my other hand as it descended. I had been practicing. "Girl me no girl," I told the hot-headed man. "Remember, I am the one who is going to find your missing mate."

"Unnatural female," he said between clenched teeth, "daughter of a bullock, I am wasting my time here." He turned on his heel—which is a dreadful and doubtful cliché, but he actually did it—and with great impetus he strode to the door. Signaling Joddy with a tilt of my head to let him go without further ado, I waited until he exited with a slam, then sheathed my dagger.

Perhaps I should admit to a slight feeling of weakness in the knees. Quite gladly I returned to my seat. Joddy approached to put the police whistle back into the Japanese bowl on my desk where such oddments reposed, and as he did so, he darted a furtive look at me.

"Thank you, Joddy, for your conspicuous gallantry," I told him, my tone assuring him that he had done right.

"I will deal with the constable if he appears, which is not likely." Reaching into a drawer for my best-quality sketching paper, I began, whilst it was still fresh in my mind, to draw the face of Wolcott Balestier as I remembered it from the photograph.

I felt Joddy's gaze upon me anxiously again, and I chose to answer his unspoken question: What was I doing?

"My best revenge for that bully's rudeness," I said, "will be to locate his missing friend for him."

• • •

When my favourite cabbie arrived to take me home that evening, pale citrine shafts of springtime sun angled through the London fog so fetchingly that I lingered, standing at the kerb for a moment to pat his horse's nose. "Hello, Brownie," I said to the horse, and to the driver, "Have you had a good day, Harold?"

"Proper sausage an' pork, miss." This, I gathered, meant that he had made good money. "Praise be," he elaborated, "the warm weather brings folk out fer a ride in the 'ansom. And how was yer day, Miss Enola?"

"Interrupted. I have not done my geometry lesson," I admitted. After the Vociferations of the Vehement

Visitor, I had utterly lost interest in conic sections, put them aside, and spent the rest of the day drawing a detailed head of "Cotswold," and also making many disrespectful sketches of his friend, the fiery client who was not a client and whose name I did not know.

"Harold," I asked, "where is Maiden Lane?"

He contorted his face and tugged at his right earlobe, pondering. "Hain't it somewhere in Charing Cross, Miss Enola?"

"Let us go see, Harold. Take me there."

"Straightaway?"

"Yes, straightaway." I got into the cab. "This very moment."

We clip-clopped off. The ride to Maiden Lane was not long. At the centre of the web of old London, Charing Cross nested, an oddly rhyming spider of main roads: the Mall, Pall Mall, Whitehall, the Strand, Northumberland. . . . Shouting inquiries at other cab-drivers, Harold drove to a part of London just off of Belford Street near the Strand.

From the airy seat of the hansom I saw crowds of well-dressed men and women on the pavements, most of them hurrying home for dinner. I saw no ragamuffin

children, beggars, or vendors; this was a genteel neighbourhood. My attention fixed at once on a woman—a
handsome woman, worthy to be called a lady really, in a
silvery silk gown, but why was she standing on the corner as if she had something to sell? Pale and statuesque
amidst natty gentlemen and ladies in flowery springtime
frocks, she appealed to all who passed, touching their
sleeves, stopping them and engaging them in the most
urgent conversation whilst showing them something.

What in the world? One did not see religious zealots
and the like in the better neighbourhoods. I simply had
to find out what she was about. But even as I lifted my
parasol to rap the roof of the cab, Harold turned a corner
onto a side street and stopped. "This be it, Miss Enola,"
he called down to me from his perch above and behind
me. "Maiden Lane."

I stepped out and turned to address him on high.
"Might you and Brownie wait a moment whilst I take
a stroll?"

"Of course, miss."

It was a nice, if narrow, street of small shops with
flats above them. I set off, but not at a strolling pace.
Briskly, like the earnest and orderly pedestrians around

me, I walked back towards the corner on which the interesting lady stood. As I neared her, I could hear her importuning voice quite clearly. "Have you at any time today seen him?"

Good heavens, she was an American! Unmistakably, by her accent. Was that why her conduct was so very eccentric?

Quite shamelessly clutching at the elbow of the gentleman ahead of me, she stopped him. "Have you seen this man? He didn't come home last night." In her other hand she displayed a large, framed photograph.

Even from a few paces away I could see it. And recognise it. Good heavens some more, it was the same fellow, the same photograph that the vehement visitor had showed me: Wolcott whatever-his-name-was. Cotswold.

I must admit I experienced a distinct sensation of glee.

The gentleman shook his head with a slight bow, then continued on his way, but quite willingly I took his place. "I beg your pardon, miss, but you say someone's gone missing?" Being taller than she was, I had to look down, peering beneath the brim of her feathery pouf of a hat to see her face.

Instantly, sympathy crowded out my glee when I saw

she was fighting back tears. For a moment she couldn't speak. Hers was not a lovely face; it was a bit too square and strong for a woman, and her proboscis was nearly as pronounced as mine, a worthy reason for me to feel even more sympathy for her.

"I'm so sorry," I said quite truthfully as she rather shakily showed me the photograph. "I haven't seen him. Is he your husband?"

"No!" Her voice trembled like her hands. "No, he is my brother! I keep house for him!"

Indeed, her face resembled that of her brother. She had the same fine skin, arched brows, speaking eyes, sweetly wide mouth.

"Good heavens!" This time I blurted it out loud. "Then he is an American too?" *Brilliant deductive reasoning, Enola,* I thought, blushing furiously at my own statement of the obvious.

But she was beyond noticing my stupidity so long as I provided a listening pair of ears. "He just went for a walk up the Strand last evening," she said, her voice quaking, "to see the lights of the Savoy Hotel, and he never . . . came . . . home."

Newfangled electric lamps, she meant. London's

latest sensation, the Savoy Hotel, had only recently opened its decadent doors. That event had included a parade of baby elephants through its courtyards flooded with that astonishing modern source of illumination. Built to be the eighth wonder of the world, the Savoy boasted electric lights throughout its tall and majestic structure, including every opulent guest room! Also, or so I had heard, it had luxurious electric heating, and even electric "ascending rooms," although exactly what those were I could not imagine.

"He went to see the new Savoy Hotel," I prompted.

"Just after dark yesterday evening, but I don't know . . . what has . . . happened to him."

Shaking my head to indicate I didn't know either, I moved on. The American lady—if that was not a contradiction in terms—the expensively dressed woman seized upon the next person who passed. "Have you seen this man? He's missing."

I doubled back to where I had left the cab and told Harold, "I am sorry to have kept you waiting." Paying him handsomely, as always, I dismissed him for the day.

He picked up the reins, but hesitated to drive away. "Miss Enola, are you sure you will be all right?"

"Of course I will be all right." I am sure my eyes were alight with my own peculiar mania, that of finding what was lost, and I could almost feel my nostrils twitching like those of a hound dog hot on a scent. "Harold," I told the avuncular cabbie with fond exasperation, "don't you remember the first time we met?" I had, with the inducement of lucre and against his better judgment, borrowed his hansom cab, his jacket, and his bowler hat, and then, smoking a cigar, I had driven Brownie off to explore London's East End, in search of clues about what had happened to a duchess who had disappeared.

He remembered, as I could see quite clearly by his heavenward glance. Then, as now, I had been on the hunt—but even so, I smiled, quite glowing in the warmth of his concern for me. My name, Enola, backwards spells "alone," and for most of my life, until lately, I had felt very much alone indeed.

Remembering, I spoke more gently. "I'll turn up eventually," I assured Harold.

And so, I hoped, if I had my way, would Wolcott Balestier.

Chapter the Second

After Harold drove off, I rather gayly sashayed, twirling my parasol, back towards the corner where Wolcott Balestier's sister continued to plead with all and sundry for information regarding her brother. Although her methods were unscientific, I had to admire her juice, and I quite wanted to help her find Cotswold, for if he was at all like his sister, I was already fond of him. Trying to observe her inconspicuously, I sauntered into a small stationer's shop where I picked up one pencil sharpener after another, each moulded more cleverly than the last, but all most likely unsatisfactory. From sad experience

I knew that one either held the sharpener and turned the pencil, or held the pencil and turned the sharpener, and almost invariably one ended up breaking the lead. Between glances at these annoying things, I watched out the front window; Miss Balestier remained at her post. Idiotically I found myself purchasing yet one more pencil sharpener (in the shape of a railway station!) to add to my collection, hoping as always that it would somehow work better than the others.

I ventured out of the stationer's and entered the next shop, a perfumery, and then, driven away by excessive bouquet, too much aroma upon fragrance upon redolent scent, I exited and continued to the next shop, a glover's. Miss Balestier remained nearby, begging of all and sundry "Have you seen this man?" From within the shop I could hear the pleading lady's voice, and luckily I quite needed (or, perhaps more accurately, wanted) a new pair of gloves to go with a lovely new puce dress; perhaps a soft grey kid? Hungrily I scanned the shelves. Jersey gloves with lace cuffs, pigskin, suede, kid, lisle cotton with dainty embroidery on the back, and—oh, the very latest thing, silk! Baby blue, ecru, jasmine, and—oh, lavender! The very latest colour.

I was just at the point of unbuttoning my trusty fawn-coloured kid gloves to be fitted for a pair when Big Ben tolled the hour, lesser bells chimed, and I glanced outside. Day was waning into twilight, and foot traffic was thinning. And making herself a bit conspicuous by her hasty, bouncing gait, up Maiden Street came a stout, middle-aged woman in the black frock and white apron of a parlour-maid, red-faced and with her lace cap askew. Her manner both impetuous and hesitant in the way of servants everywhere when they have worked up the courage to intervene, she halted, panting, and addressed the American lady. "Please, Miss Balestier," she wheedled, "please come back inside now before you catch your death of cold." The parlour-maid's appearance and her accent were not American at all, but stoutly working-class British. Like a great English sheep-dog, guiding but not touching, the parlour-maid tried to herd Miss Balestier away from her corner.

But the lady in silver silk took no notice of her at all. Remaining in the same place, she continued to cry out, "Have you seen this gentleman? He is missing!" as before to the strangers who passed.

New gloves forgotten, I exited the shop to watch—

just as a younger, lesser maid came running up Maiden Street in her turn, carrying a white lace wrap. Together, the two women quite gently attempted to place this inadequate garment around the lady's shoulders, but, indifferent and unfocused, she shrugged it off.

Wide-eyed, the maids looked at each other, and in whispers they conferred. Then the elder one bustled off. Discreetly following, I made note of the Maiden Street address to which she returned, hoping it would prove to be that of the missing man.

A moment after the parlour-maid went in, a boy came dashing out, and away, with such a warrior mien on his pug-nosed face that I deduced he had been sent on an important errand.

My abdominal region let out a rebellious and wolfish growl. Quite sternly I shushed it. Hunger would have to wait, for either notable events were imminent or I was a nincompoop. Slipping back towards Miss Balestier, I positioned myself in the lengthening shadows beside the glover's shop to wait for whatever might happen next.

The lady still stood like a statue on her corner, her pale face even more desperate than before as she displayed her brother's likeness to the uncaring night. Fewer gentlemen and ladies now were passing, but a motley circle of onlookers ranging from posh to pauper had formed around her. I heard some sympathetic murmurs.

". . . clear off 'er 'ead."

". . . case of a broken 'eart . . ."

"Where's 'er 'usband? Or 'er father?"

". . . should be under a doctor's care."

The lady's lacy shawl remained on the pavement, and quite a shabby elderly woman limped forwards, picked it up, and with some difficulty replaced it around Miss Balestier's shoulders. My heart was touched at the sight of such humble solicitude, and I quite had to restrain myself from rushing forwards to minister some kindness of my own—but I remained where I was, telling myself that, unless I was very much mistaken, something would happen soon.

The pale lady stood out like an alabaster distress signal in the gloaming, utterly unaware of the onlookers, her strong-boned face stark with misery, eyes staring into nowhere.

Peripherally I noticed that something else quite white in the dusk was approaching.

I stared. Striding up Maiden Lane came a gentleman resplendent in white tie, white waistcoat, white orchid in his buttonhole, the tails of his cutaway flying like oriflammes as he progressed to the rescue. "Carrie," he called, "Caroline, it's time for good girls to come inside," his tone only slightly sardonic. Still, I recognised his voice.

Egad. In reaction, I plastered my personage even deeper into concealing shadows, for the newcomer was the selfsame bristling lummox who had accosted me in my office that afternoon.

The lady—Caroline—widened her staring eyes and seemed to focus them, turning her head slowly towards him as he walked up to stand beside her.

"Ye gods, woman," he said in a tender, playful way I would not have believed of him, "staying out here in the nasty, darkling chilly-fingered twilight, have you no more brain than a parsnip?" I could see his face now, and although teasing, he was somehow not making fun of her.

Her voice low and faltering, she said, "I cannot just sit and do nothing, Ruddy."

Was that his name? It suited him, because I knew he could be ruddy rude.

But he wasn't being a baboon at the moment. "Carrie, dear, please come in." He offered his arm like a gentleman.

She hesitated. "Did you secure . . . that doctor. . . ."

"Ragostin? No, he turned out to be a fraud, the veriest charlatan, but I engaged someone else quite respictibibble." Still playful, no doubt trying to cheer her, he started mimicking an Irish accent. "Carrie, me love, come hoome. Sure and it's a spictacle ye're afther makin' uv yerself out here, and me supposed to be a-dancin' wif grand lydies and such."

"Oh, Ruddy, I'm so sorry!" Sounding as if she meant it, she took his arm and let him lead her away. "I never thought—I forgot—they called you away from your *fate*?"

"Sure and there's always another fate, Caroleen me colleen," he blarneyed, escorting her step by steady step towards the Maiden Lane doorway where the parlour-maid waited.

Fate? I wondered as I turned to make my way

"hoome." What sort of fate could this Ruddy man have and be called away from?

. . .

The next morning at the ruddy crack of dawn, a tall but timid, very plain-faced and shabby pauper girl dared to knock at the servants' door of the Balestier residence, shivering in the chill of springtime weather turned cold again, and asking in a Cockney accent whether there might be a job of work for her there, in exchange for food and a penny.

'Twas I. Wanting to know a great deal more about Wolcott Balestier and the circumstances of his disappearance, I had dirtied my face and donned nostril inserts to broaden my proboscis, stained my teeth brown, and knuckled my eyes to bruise them just a little bit and make them tearful. I had purposely neglected to braid my hair the night before, so that as I slept it would become tangled, and I wore it hanging loose and unkempt. In addition, I had rendered every part of my personage grimy and ragged, with old brogues splitting wide open on my otherwise bare feet. Indeed, as I exited the Charing

Cross Underground station and made my way to Maiden Lane, I feared—judging from the way other people shied away from me—that I might have taken my disguise a bit too far, might have overshot "poor thing" and, instead, achieved "a dreadful fright"!

But the maid who came to the door did not shy away, not at all. Instead, she sent the boy for the doughty parlour-maid, who looked, this morning, quite the worse for wear. After having the under-maid inspect me for fleas and lice, the parlour-maid was glad enough to welcome me in. It was just as I had surmised: the Balestier household had been knocked topsy-turvy by the mysterious failure of the master to return for yet another night; there had been much coming and going, the lady had needed extra care, and yesterday's dinner dishes had not been washed. I soon found myself scrubbing them with ferocious lye soap that burned my hands, turning those appendages an appropriately ugly red.

The cook, a stout and swarthy woman wielding a cast-iron skillet of mixed leftovers, came over to scald the clean dishes with a kettle full of boiling water before the maid-of-all-work dried them. "It don't make no sense," the cook told the maid. "What's a person to think could have happened? Master was chipper enough at dinner, weren't he?"

Oho! My ears hearkened greedily, but I trust I gave no visible sign of how ardently I was listening.

"Nuffin weighing on his mind when he left for his walk," the maid agreed.

"What the missus is on and on about, book pirates grabbed him, I don't believe it."

Pirates again, but *book* pirates?

The cook shook her heavy head. "It cain't be that dangerous of a business, books."

"A person wouldn't think so," said the maid in a tone that implied that perhaps "a person" would. "What with them being American and all."

Of this interesting topic they spoke no more, for a different maid came into the kitchen; I heard her enter and set a tray on the table. "How is the missus?" the cook demanded.

"She's that upset, she didn't touch her egg and soldiers nor 'er crumpet neither," the other replied. "All she took was pear butter on toast, and 'ardly 'alf a slice of that."

"Poor lady, she's proper prostrated."

"Wretched enough to want breakfast in bed, but she intends on getting up now."

The not-for-mistress breakfast heating on the skillet made a strange bubbling, squeaking noise, and the cook hurried back to it. "Sit down," she ordered, serving a portion. Others came in, and I stole a look; this was a modest household of only three maids and a boy, and few if any of them slept in, for the Balestiers occupied only a flat, although a good-sized one.

I kept on scrubbing dishes, and the cook kept on adding more to the sink already full of them, but after the others had hurried through their breakfast and gone, she ordered me, "Dry yer 'ands, roll down yer sleeves, and sit." She had saved me a goodly portion of the thrifty household breakfast, and I found it not at all difficult to act my pauper part; I bolted it down.

Then there were the breakfast dishes for me to wash, the tables to be wiped clean, and the slop bucket to be emptied, and then the cook turned me over to the parlour-maid. Once I left the warmth of the kitchen, I found it nearly as chilly inside the house as it was out-doors, for no fires could be lit until the fireplaces were cleaned. All the ash from the evening before had to be disposed of. Equipped with an entire stack of metal buckets, a clumsy, scoop-like shovel, and a short broom, I made my rounds: front parlour, back parlour, dining room, library, bedroom (whilst Miss Balestier was in the dressing room and the maids were making the bed), and the other bedroom, which belonged of course to Wolcott Balestier.

My ears perked up, so to speak, when I entered this bedroom, and I took time and care to look around me. The arsenic-green wallpaper crawling with acanthus leaves was nearly covered (quite wisely, I thought) with pictures, many of them framed and titled photographs: Rochester, New York, a city appearing to be more of stone than brick, with the Erie Canal running through it. This interesting and watery subject was presented from several different views. Also on Mr. Balestier's bedroom wall was a large photograph of a stern-looking, lantern-jawed woman called Susan B. Anthony.

The name was familiar to me. Hmm. Was she not an American leader of the Suffragist movement?

I began to form a favourable opinion of Wolcott Balestier. A look at his escritoire showed me that he had untidy, whimsical, thoroughly charming handwriting.

Also, judging by some figurines and yet more pictures, he quite liked dogs. Numerous coloured and labeled lithographs depicted various American breeds of dogs, such as a round-headed Boston Bull Terrier, a fluffy white Eskimo Dog, and various hounds: Coon hound, Plott hound, Leopard hound—surely they did not hunt leopards in America? I could not at the moment think upon what continent leopards were found, and I was interrupted by the return of the parlour-maid.

Under her close supervision, I then laid the fires, placing upon the hearth in each room small kindling, then larger sticks, all tented over a fir cone soaked in paraffin, then a small log and some coal on top. There was more to laying a fire than I had realised.

After that, left on my own to follow orders, I again progressed from chamber to chamber, cleaning and tidying the fire tongs, large poker, small poker, et cetera in their stands. And then, with my abdominal region already yowling for luncheon, I collected all the coal scuttles from each room, took them down to the coal bin in the basement, and filled them, after which I was required to carry each one, now heavy, separately back to its domain.

The library, which doubled as an office, was empty, and I took the opportunity to filch several interesting-looking documents from what appeared to be Wolcott Balestier's desk. I folded these small and concealed them on my shabby personage. Then I went back to fetch the last scuttle of coal.

Lugging the weighty thing towards the parlour, I recognised the troubled voice of Miss Balestier issuing from within. It would seem, therefore, that she had a visitor.

". . . shamefully not bound by international copyright agreements, you see," she was explaining, or trying to explain, her voice unsteadily on the verge of tears. "They are ruthless in their greed. Munro is the worst. . . ."

As she faltered, a man's sharp, cultured voice took over. "An American tycoon can scarcely be expected to resist British lucre ripe for the plucking," said he just as I opened the parlour door and stepped in.

I very nearly shrieked, dropped the coal, and ran. One could not mistake the precise tones of Sherlock Holmes, and my animal instincts remembered all too well how, in previous years, I had fled from him because he wanted to capture and civilise me. But there was no need to run away *now*, and anyhow, he would not see through my disguise, I reassured myself. This had always proved true in the past.

Meanwhile, Sherlock kept speaking in his usual didactic manner. "But, as I understand what you have told me, the John W. Lovell Company felt that wrong was being done, and therefore sent your brother to England specifically to right it."

I continued into the parlour, heaving my load of coal towards the fireplace, careful to look only at my destination.

"Of course," said Miss Balestier as strongly as she was able. "It's the only moral thing to do. But I never thought, I could not imagine, that simply doing the right thing might put his life at risk!"

Sherlock replied, but I have no idea at all what he said at that moment, for I *felt* him recognise me. Absolute knowledge that he had done so pierced me like a dart in the back of my neck. As I set down the coal scuttle and turned around, I exhorted myself, *Enola, you will carry this off quite well,* and forced myself to glance at him. Sure enough, his hawklike gaze was on me. Our eyes met, and I gave him just the hint of a nod. Not even blinking, he looked away from me at once and continued to speak to his client—for surely his client Miss Balestier must be.

("I engaged someone else quite respictibibble," the Ruddy man had said with a mock Irish accent. Sure now and begorrah, he had—the great Sherlock Holmes, who usually took no interest in missing persons.)

Rather gently, for him, Sherlock asked Miss Balestier, "Have you called in Scotland Yard?"

"Yes, but they said my brother had only been gone less than a day. . . ." Her voice broke, but then she went on quickly, all but sobbing, "Truly, you must find my brother, Mr. Holmes! Having a child go missing could not be any worse. Wolcott is such an old soul and yet such a sensitive innocent, with such lofty ideals, such quick sympathy. . . ." Quite quietly, before she had finished, I exited the parlour and closed the door behind me, thinking of Wolcott Balestier's eager, finely chiseled face I had never actually seen, yet knew: brilliant eyes, puckish ears, wide and presumably mobile mouth—I quite liked him.

I sighed. Good odours of sausage and pudding wafted from the kitchen, seducing my innards, but I allowed myself no pause. Forsaking my luncheon and the penny I might have earned, I exited another door, the servants' door to the Balestier residence, and immediately started shivering in my rags; although it was nearly May, winter seemed to have returned. Indeed, desultory snowflakes fell from a leaden sky as I made my way around the side of the building and huddled behind a corner near the front, waiting for Sherlock.

Chapter the Third

A cab also waited for him, its enclosed carriage surely warmer than the open air, but being a wretch of a pauper today, I knew better than to approach the driver asking to be let in. He would have chased me away with his whip. If I had sprinted up and down Maiden Lane, I could have kept myself warmer, but would have made myself conspicuous, whereas I quite wanted to escape notice from the Balestier household. Therefore, with martyred devotion to my chosen perditorial profession, I waited, hands tucked beneath my arms, the remainder of my personage quaking with chill.

At last Sherlock came out and strode down the front walk. Unceremoniously I bolted for the cab and got to it ahead of him, letting myself in. The cab-driver yelped, but Sherlock hushed him with a gesture, then took off his greatcoat and placed it over me like a blanket before he seated himself by my side. "221 Baker Street," he told the driver, and of me he demanded, "Aren't you supposed to be in school, Enola?"

Huddled beneath his woolen charity, I gave him no answer but a sour look.

"Why are you here?" My brother raised his voice, if only to be heard above the clamour of cab wheels growling on cobbles. "Who is your client?" As, once again, I did not answer, he verbally dissected his own question. "I am assisting Miss Balestier. Surely neither she nor Mr. Balestier hired you. Who did?" His tone sharpened. "Enola, please tell me that you are not spying for the enemy!"

Stung, I retorted, "Of course not! I give you my word I am not." Of what enemy did he speak? Who or what on earth were book pirates? "You think Long John Silver has him?"

Sherlock stared at me as if questioning my senses.

I sighed. "I take it that you do not read the novels of Robert Louis Stevenson."

"No, not those or any other novels."

"Your loss. By 'Long John Silver,' I refer to all this nonsense about pirates, Sherlock."

"It's not nonsense." Seeing an opportunity to educate me, he took it with alacrity, but in such strident tones that I shall spare the gentle reader all but the gist: the term "book pirates" referred to American publishers, such as this Munro person, who reprinted the diligent handiwork of English writers and sold it far and wide without recompensing the authors so much as a penny. No wonder they called it piracy. Wolcott Balestier worked for just such an American publisher, the John W. Lovell Company, which had either grown a conscience (if such an entity can be said to do so) or seen an opportunity, because said Company had sent Balestier to London to contract with such English authors for their novels *in advance,* offering them some money, even if only a small amount.

"Thus, you see, he threatened the piracy of the other publishers, who may well have seen fit to do away with him!" declared Sherlock.

"Merely because of money?" It seemed hardly a murdering matter to me. "Have you any proof?"

"Enola, I've only just started my investigation! And I ask you again, how is this your concern?"

I shrugged off the question and distracted him with one of my own. "How did you recognise me, back there in the Balestier residence?" I demanded.

He parried, "How did you *know* I recognised you?"

"I felt your stare boring into the back of my skull! How did you know that ragamuffin was me?" It had been easy enough for me to fool him in the past.

He answered, "Why, by that selfsame dolichocephalic skull of yours, and your famously marshy hair, and your scarecrow gait, and . . ." He paused, thinking, then added almost apologetically, "It would seem I have gotten to know you a great deal better since last summer, Enola."

No sensible reply occurred to me, so I kept silence, feeling now much warmer, thanks no doubt to his greatcoat.

Sherlock, also, seemed to have nothing more to say for the moment. The cab was pulling to a halt, and, blinking, I realised we had arrived at 221 Baker Street. Squirming out from under Sherlock's coat and handing it back to him, I said, "Would you kindly direct the cabbie to take me home to the Women's Club?"

"Do you think they will let you in, looking like that?"

"By the kitchen door, yes." While most of the members of the Club never saw me otherwise than in proper attire, the servants knew me better. I was still much wont to roam the night, sometimes to distribute charity, sometimes to explore London as a midden-picker. "The staff have grown accustomed to my eccentricities."

Sherlock rolled his eyes. "Then kindly go straight to bed and stay there for the next few days, lest you catch pneumonia."

All innocence, I inquired, "But what about school?"

"Bah," he said, getting out of the cab and closing its door rather harder than seemed necessary. Presumably he paid the cab-driver. I could hear him giving my requested instructions, and I felt myself smiling.

. . .

Once back in my room at the Professional Women's Club, I shed my dreadful clothing and ordered a hip bath, which I took in front of a blessedly comforting fire. Then, in my warm dressing-gown, I ate a late luncheon from a tray. (Coincidentally, it was sausage and pudding.) I did not, however, then go to bed, kindly or otherwise. Heaven forbid I should do what my brother told me to. Instead, I examined the papers I had filched from the Balestier library. They all seemed to be either typewritten letters or copies done with carbonic paper, and from his elegantly printed letterhead I learned that Wolcott Balestier was Editor-in-Chief of *Tid Bits* magazine at the John W. Lovell Company in New York City.

Tid Bits magazine? I had never heard of it.

Sighing, I sat at my vanity/desk/art table, reached for paper and pencil, and began to write one of my habitual lists:

> Find out more about the John W. Lovell Company
> Find out who, exactly, is Munro?
> How are these book pirates best challenged? In terms of headquarters, manufactory, distribution
> Where are their operatives located in England?

Staring at these questions, I realised that simply applying logic to them and pondering their ramifications would get me nowhere; I needed data, as Sherlock would say. I needed information. First thing in the morning I would inquire of the librarian at my Women's Academy—

No, I wouldn't! "Blast and confound!" I exclaimed, pencil falling from my vexed fingers. "First thing in the morning" the Academy would be locked and lifeless, for tomorrow was Sunday. London's new Subscription Library would be closed. The newspaper and publishing offices on Fleet Street would be closed. Even my favourite refuge and source of information would not welcome me on a Sunday, that being the Hyde Park home of Florence Nightingale. Yes, *the* Florence Nightingale, quite elderly now and housebound, but still splendidly advised of societal causes and current events.

But as I could not see her on the sabbath, I cast about in my mind for others . . . could I consult fellow members of the Professional Women's Club? Or perhaps my friends Tish and Flossie Glover? Or my other very best friend, Lady Cecily Alistair? Alas, she was still in Europe, but perhaps her lovely mother, Lady Theodora Alistair?

No. None of them seemed likely to know anything of these matters about which I needed to educate myself.

Perhaps on Monday I could disguise myself and seek employment with some magazine where someone might know of Lovell or *Tid Bits* . . . but no, no, such investigative devices were too slow. "Cotswold" should be found sooner rather than later. In that regard, I found that I shared Caroline Balestier's sense of urgency.

"Carrie," the bristle-faced, bespectacled man had called her. Ruddy, she had called him. Scowling at the thought of him, I retrieved my pencil and wrote more questions:

Who is my client who is not a client?
Is he a factor in his friend's disappearance?
What is his fate of which Caroline Balestier spoke?

I sighed, looked out my window, saw that already the cold, grey day was waning, and reached for the bell-pull.

"You may take the tray," I told the maid when she answered my summons, "and please, send someone to help me civilise my hair. At once."

Cotswold had been gone for two days. Something must be done. For the time being, I must needs leave the learned inquiries to Sherlock, but I had thought of another possibility I could explore.

I could try to see whether Wolcott Balestier had possibly got into any trouble between his home and the Savoy.

. . .

Shortly after dark, at approximately the same time as Wolcott Balestier must have done Thursday, I started walking from Maiden Lane down Southampton Street towards the Strand. Unlike earlier today, I had exercised the good sense to dress warmly, but still I looked humble, if not downright dowdy, in my very oldest boots and cardigan sweater. I wore my hair braided and "up," I had concealed my hands in an old-fashioned muff (the gentle reader will kindly bear with this eccentricity, being soon to learn the reason for it), and as a final thumb in the nose at stylishness, I had tied a shawl over my head. I flattered myself that the poor would not be afraid of me, but the well-to-do might yet condescend to speak with me.

If, after all, I encountered any people of either persuasion! These Charing Cross streets did not throng after dark as those of the East End did; here dwelt populace with proper homes who stayed safely indoors at night. On Southampton Street, which only hours ago had bustled with shoppers and pedestrians, with cabs and carriages, with "orderly boys" who scuttled about, plying scoops and buckets, beneath the very hooves of the horses, trying to pick up their all-too-frequent deposits—on Southampton Street now, effluvium of such equine deposits remained, but street and pavements lay mostly empty except for a few passing cabs, no doubt bound for the theatre.

Only a straggle of pedestrians trudged towards me, mere shadows or silhouettes in the meager gaslight. But I knew who they were. I could make out their forlorn gaits, their lumpy shapes: men in caps and baggy trousers, women in shawls, nary a top hat nor a fancy bonnet to be seen. They were trampers. People without homes, during the day they slept, sitting upright, on the benches along the Embankment. The law was that they had to sit up, giving an appearance of decorum, or they would be told by a constable to move on. To lie down, in a churchyard or under an awning or anywhere, was to risk being arrested for vagrancy. And at night, the law's mandate was that the City streets be kept clear of "rough sleepers" altogether. So, during the dark hours, they tramped ceaselessly, hungry and hopeless. In a way, this wealthier part of London was more hostile to the poor than the East End. There, ministering at night in the guise of the Sister of the Streets, I had found the poor starving or freezing at their leisure. Here, they had to walk all night.

Standing under a streetlight so as to be quite visible, I let my muff drop to the pavement, and, my hands indecorously bare of gloves, I began to juggle four pennies in the air. (Juggling was one of several disreputable skills I had been practicing during hours I might have better spent learning my geometry.) I used pennies because all of those who were watching knew one penny would buy someone a place sitting in a warm room all night, although he or she would not be allowed to sleep. Two pennies would buy a night in a warm room sleeping whilst sitting up and resting head and shoulders on a rope. Four pennies would buy a meal (a chunk of bread, a cup of tea) and a night's sleep in a "coffin" on the floor of a reasonably warm doss-house. I suspected fourpence was a fortune to these folk.

Evidently they thought so, too. Every single one of them slowed to a stop, staring at me.

Eyes on my whirling pennies so as not to alarm any of the onlookers, I spoke. "Did you pass this way two nights ago?" Because most people, even the very poor, were creatures of habit, I hoped so.

"Aye," said a man's gruff Yorkshire voice, and "Yis," said a Cockney woman.

"Did you see anything out of the usual? A man's gone missing. I want to know what happened to him."

"Wot sort o' man?" said both in unison.

"A gentleman, young, clean-shaven, with the face of an angel." I ceased my juggling, catching two pennies in each hand, and I gave them to the man and woman who were talking to me. Then I picked up my muff, and from inside it, I pulled a picture of Cotswold I had drawn on very white paper with black, black India ink so that anyone with reasonable eyesight could see it even in the lamplight.

Of the trampers who had stopped to watch me juggle, most moved on. Some stayed to beg for pennies, and a few, including those who had spoken, crowded closer to look at my rendition of Cotswold's face.

"'At's 'im," said the woman, a plain, aging soul with frizzy hair escaping her head-scarf. "A top-'at he wore, and 'e nodded at us pleasant-like."

"And then?"

"Then 'e walked on 'is way." She gestured behind her, towards the Strand. "A-swinging 'is cane."

"Aye," agreed the gruff man.

"Headin' fer the dog-fight," someone else said with a hollow laugh. A poor joke, I thought, as I gave out pennies all around, for only the lowest class of East End ruffians went to dog-fights. Tucking both Cotswold's picture and my hands back into my capacious muff, I walked onwards, towards the Strand and any other people I could accost.

Chapter the Fourth

By the time, quite late in the evening, when I finally reached the Savoy, I had spoken with (and given pennies to) many more trampers. I had also spoken to (but withheld gratuities from) several extraordinarily tarted-up women loitering on street-corners, which legally, as "necessary social evils," they were quite permitted to do, although poor folk stopping to catch their breath were ordered to move on.

I questioned the "ladies of the night," and some of them had seen Cotswold two evenings ago. Indeed, they had noticed him particularly because, in their opinion, he was quite handsome. He had passed them by, they said, without a smile but not with a scowl of superiority, either.

Besides the "fallen women," the only other rightfully employed female I spoke with was a "Hallelujah Lassie" of the so-called Salvation Army, a "soldier" in her blue serge uniform and old-fashioned black straw bonnet strictly tied in a huge funereal bow beneath her surprisingly formidable chin. Her close-set eyes, however, were meek. She had not seen Cotswold, but earnestly she cautioned me against a large Alsatian dog that had been roaming the area a couple of nights before.

The word "dog" echoed in my mind. What was it one of the trampers had said about a dog-fight? Such deplorable canine combats were frequent in the East End, but not here in the City of London, where pets were many but stray dogs were few, for the police had no more mercy for them than they did for human strays. Neither destitute dogs nor penniless paupers marred the neighbourhood of the Savoy.

And as I neared that landmark and its famous electric lights, I found myself drawn to their brilliance like a moth, momentarily forgetting all about Wolcott Balestier. The entire eight-storey bulk of the Savoy Hotel and Restaurant was visible as if creating its own sunrise in the night, with its great arched double entrance, its fountains, its statuary, its tiers of balconies framed in Art Nouveau fretwork, all arrayed in glittering luminescence. For the first time, although from the opposite pavement of the Strand, I experienced the brilliance of electric crystal chandeliers, the ones I glimpsed coruscating from within the great hotel, their hanging prisms augmenting their white incandescence almost beyond belief. I stood gawking and blinking at the scene before me: like an array of fine china figurines in a shop, elegant couples seated at snowy tables seemed on display behind the many windows of the lambent dining room. Many more such couples swanned within the great entry hall. And quite a press of elegant carriages came and went, drawn by the most shining of horses, to deliver an astonishing number of fine people being shown in by an equally astonishing number of uniformed footmen.

Some illustrious event, I mused. What could it be?

The answer seemed to be on display beside the stately doors. There I saw quite a large placard presenting, amidst a great deal of gold leaf, an oversized photograph of a man with a pugnacious air: jutting chin, a veritable scrub-brush of a moustache, beetling eyebrows to match, and—

And I recognised him. Good heavens, it was Ruddy. What the ruddy blazes was going on?

From my discreet distance I peered at the gold lettering surrounding and glorifying Ruddy's bespectacled face, but by its highly decorative nature it was difficult to make out. I did manage to decipher the largest and most prominent word: FETE.

Oh, gingersnaps! I felt ineffably stupid; Ruddy's fate was a fete.

But why was he being so honoured? Who was he?

Knowing I risked looking like an ill-clad burdock amidst a rosy posy of expensively gowned womanhood, I crossed the Strand and ventured towards the front of the hotel to find out. Stopping just short of the crowd outside the Savoy, squinting, I managed to read:

FETE

HOSTED BY

LADY SOPHRONIA, MARCHIONESS OF SUMATTERBURY

IN HONOUR OF

POET, AUTHOR, MAN OF LETTERS, and CHAMPION OF EMPIRE.

But the name that followed was obscured from my view by shoulders and heads, both male and female heads, many and mightily hatted.

I hesitated to approach any nearer, because tending the doors were several redoubtable footmen in resplendent uniform, and they were likely to shoo me away. My curiosity would have to wait, for the important question, I reminded myself vehemently, did not concern the identity of this high pooh-bah with the overgrown moustache; rather it concerned whatever had become of his "best friend a man ever had," Wolcott Balestier.

I must continue to ask.

Scanning a crowd of gawkers, I spotted at some distance up the Strand a genteel sort of woman selling flowers arrayed upon a large tray slung from her neck. Selling boutonnieres, actually, consisting of red or white carnations, blue cornflowers, or creamy gardenias. I started towards her just as a couple of her customers

concluded their business and turned away: a pair of gentlemen dressed to the utmost in white tie and tails. As
they walked past me, tucking their posies into their but-
tonholes and giving each other glances in which I saw
amusement, one asked the other, "Do you like kippling?"

"I don't know," said he. "I've never kippled."

They chuckled, and by their air of conspiracy together I gathered that this was a joke of some sort, but
I—

Wait. Wafting into my mind, from some headline I
had recently read, drifted a name: Rudyard Kipling.

Rudyard? What sort of ruddy name was that?

Ruddy??

I heard one of the gentlemen say to the other, ". . .
some sort of literary type, just returned from years in
India and abroad. He's caught on tremendously of late."

"So my wife says," returned the other. "She's making
me . . ." *Attend the fete,* I guessed, as I could no longer
hear them.

Rudyard. Kipling. Kippling; didn't that mean salting
and smoking fish to preserve it? No, that was kippering.

Making unwritten note of the name, I tucked it away
in the back of my mind as I approached the woman selling

boutonnieres, a stout but severely corseted woman of a certain age whose nose, I noticed, was the opposite of mine; hers was oddly flat, as if her face had gone through a press sometime early in life. As if to compensate for the nose, her smile seemed wide and welcoming. She was glad, I thought at the time, to see another woman like herself—unlovely, that is—approaching.

I smiled back quite sincerely. "How do you do?" I asked—an absurd question, when one thinks about it; do what? I waited for no answer. "A bit chilly for this time of year, isn't it?"

"Gelid!" she responded with feeling. "Hyperboreal!"

What a pleasant surprise; here was someone else who gloried in vocabulary! "Brumal?" I responded, beaming. "Arctic? Glacial?"

"All of the above, and then just plain cold on top of it." She rubbed her hands together; perhaps because she needed to handle money, she wore only very thin gloves.

"Here." Impulsively I offered my muff. "Warm your poor fingers in this."

But just at that moment, somewhere behind me a man gave a horrible shout. And someone screamed—no, everyone screamed. The flat-faced woman forsook her smile to shriek, her stretched, white-rimmed eyes glaring past me, and I turned to see—

Help! Divine intervention help me!

A mad dog.

Far too near to me, and staggering nearer!

Would that electric lights were not so bright, that I could have seen it less plainly! A shadowy hint of a rabid dog would have been terrible enough. But I saw it in every dreadful detail: bristling black fur, eyes like coals of green fire, a white tide of foam spewing from its roaring, snarling mouth. Barely twenty feet away from me, it staggered and surged, attacking lamp posts, carriage wheels, anything and everything. All the people on the street cried out and fled, and no wonder, for being bitten by a dog with hydrophobia was a death sentence! I could hardly imagine a worse calamity. My dagger could not defend me from this. Screaming as heartily as anyone, I dropped my muff and ran for the nearest tree, arboreal creature that I am.

It was not a large tree, but it sufficed. I swarmed up its skinny trunk, perched in its branches (quite bare at this time of year), took a deep breath, and looked down on a thoroughfare swiftly emptying, although the Savoy, a small distance away and set back from the Strand, seemed undisturbed. But amidst all the roaring and shrieking around me, I became aware of the boutonniere woman scrabbling at the tree trunk below me in panic whilst the mad dog, a black Alsatian, veered closer. Flattening myself on the sturdiest branch, I reached down and grabbed her by the hand, yelling, "Brace your feet against the trunk!" Evidently, I observed as I hoisted her, she had never climbed a tree. But somehow, with my assistance, she struggled up to a perch beside me, where she clung safely out of reach of the slavering beast.

It actually sank its fangs into the bark of the tree we were in, gnashing at the living wood, before it passed directly beneath us, nightmarishly large and dark, a tragic travesty of every dog I had ever loved. My companion whimpered and hid her face against the tree trunk.

Sympathetic, I shouted above the hullabaloo, "I wish somebody would shoot it!"

She quavered, "A couple of nights ago a brave gentleman tried to club it with his cane, but it tore his leg open."

"A couple of nights ago!" I echoed, astonished, for I had not yet learned that animals—or people!—with hydrophobia can rampage for as many as ten days. "The same dog?"

Regaining some spirit, she retorted, "I should hope there's not more than one!"

Quiet was returning to the street, for the danger seemed to have passed. Lifting her head, my companion deployed her protective vocabulary. "Frightfully malevolent beast of a dog!"

"Monstrous," I agreed.

"Sinister!"

"Nefarious."

"Oh, well." She took a deep breath. "What has become of my things?" She peered down between the branches of our saviour tree, as did I.

"There," I said, pointing. Not far away lay her tray, her scattered flowers, my muff, and faceup on the tray, my black-and-white rendition of Wolcott Balestier.

My flat-faced friend gasped as if she had been dealt a blow, crying, "Where did that come from?"

"Where did what come from?"

"That picture! It's, um, it's him! I mean, it is he!"

"It is whom?"

"It's that man himself and no other! The one with the cane, the one that got bit by the mad dog!"

• • •

With some difficulty, I restrained myself from questioning her until after getting her down from the tree and helping her collect her belongings. But then I applied myself to ferreting all possible information out of her, and the minute I had done so (or so I thought), I hailed a cab and urged the driver to hurry to 221 Baker Street.

Alas, Mrs. Hudson, answering the door, informed me that Mr. Holmes was not in.

Blast and confound him! How dare he?

However, Mrs. Hudson urged me to come inside, out of the unseasonable chill, and sit with her by the fire in her parlour, where I penciled a message for the great detective, thus:

> *My Dear but Absent Brother,*
> *On this past Thursday evening, an amazingly educated (at least in terms of vocabulary) boutonniere vendor*
> *her name Miss Ethel Etheridge*
> *her age 27*
> *her residence 301 Brosna Terrace, Southwark,*
> *witnessed a large, black Alsatian dog running mad*

on the Strand a block west of the Savoy Hotel. She saw a gentleman she identified as Wolcott Balestier bravely attempt to dispatch it with his walking stick, and she says the mad dog "nearly tore his leg off." The location of the attack was one block behind the Savoy. The Etheridge woman does not know what became of Balestier after he was bitten because, quite sensibly, she fled the scene.

I need not tell you that, if this gentleman has indeed been so injured, his situation is so deadly that he perhaps may have taken leave of his senses, or he may have been committed to care or otherwise been unable to contact his sister. I hope that, notwithstanding tomorrow's being the Sabbath, you will be able to confer with your contacts on the police force as to where he might be, and in what condition. Meanwhile, tonight is by no means over, and I plan to return to the vicinity of the attack to seek more information.

I do hope you are doing something worthwhile.

Sincerely,
Enola

Attaching this with a push-pin to the door of Sherlock's flat so that he would be sure to receive it at the first opportunity, I took hasty leave of Mrs. Hudson, knowing that I had a great deal to do.

You see, gentle reader, having been unable to contact my brother, I considered that I should at the very least contact Ruddy, a.k.a. Rudyard Kipling.

I had not the faintest idea where he lived, but I did know, most fortunately and temporarily, where he was to be found at that time. I knew that he was presently at the Savoy Hotel and would most likely remain there until the wee hours.

From the signage surrounding that edifice, I had gathered that his fete had been running for a week, and its final night was tonight, Saturday.

Therefore, this was an opportunity I quite needed to seize, but I had just barely enough time in which to transform myself in such a way that I would be allowed to enter that magnificent edifice, find him, and speak with him.

Chapter the Fifth

I owned no ball dress or evening gown; why would I? Therefore, once upstairs in my room at the Professional Women's Club, I threw myself into hasty improvisation. Snatching from my wardrobe a favourite long and flowing creamy silk dress with leg-of-mutton sleeves and a high puffed collar, I sacrificed it, amputating with a pair of shears the aforementioned members plus a great deal of fabric in the region of my collarbone and upper back. Feverishly I snipped away until I had achieved the U-shaped exhibit of feminine immodesty known as "corsage," which would bare me nearly to my shoulders.

Then, like a predatory animal, I turned upon another favourite dress and savaged it, cutting off pale pink tiers of tulle. It took only a minute, a needle, and some white thread to baste the tulle in folds covering the rough edges of the silk dress's new neckline, creating quite a flowing and fashionable "bertha" all round.

Inspired, and desperately needing to do something about my head, I quickly and creatively tucked the rest of the tulle into the posterior interstices of my hair until I had made an artistic pouf of myself. Then, after putting on my very finest fawn-coloured boots and tightening my corset (in that order, for one cannot bend over to address one's feet in a fully tightened corset), I got into my new "gown" and evaluated my appearance in the standing mirror.

Oh, dear; in daytime one must cover every inch of skin, letting never a peep of it show between cuff and glove, but at night—!!! Bare of collarbones and shoulders, I felt terribly exposed—although I had very little frontal projection to flaunt—and terribly unprotected and defenseless without my usual baggage of supplies masquerading as such. I did, however, still have my corset and therefore my dagger, its jeweled hilt standing like a good and faithful soldier in the middle of my minimal bosom. And, I told myself fiercely, not every female had to be a goddess. With a few more touches I would pass muster.

But oh, those touches! I ran out into the hallway and ricocheted from door to door, knocking frantically, then gabbling to the women who emerged. By that time, I had lodged in my club for nearly a year, and my upstairs neighbours had grown to know me, seldom elevating their eyebrows anymore. The older woman next door, who wrote an advice column for *The Daily Chronicle*, loaned me the requisite pair of lacy long gloves extending to above my elbows. Her neighbour, who specialised in the phrenology of horses, provided the loveliest Spanish-style fan hand-painted with blush roses. And the Hydrotherapeutic Mesmerist across the hall supplied the equally requisite fox-fur wrap, more than merely decorative on this cold evening. Others outfitted me with a cascade of necklaces to cover my dagger's hilt, adding rather painful clamp-on earbobs to match. Thanking them profusely, I ran back downstairs and out to my waiting cab, with all of them waving me on my way from the windows, calling "Good luck!"

"Armed and ready!"

"You look ravishing!"

And, belatedly, "Wait, where's your escort?"

Indeed, my lack of escort might prove to be a problem.

But as it turned out, I entered the Savoy Hotel simply by slipping in with a gaggle of other women, aunts and nieces and cousins and such, attending as a family led by a single patriarchal male.

Once inside the vast foyer, I slowed to a halt, very conscious of the magnificent coffered ceiling simply because I could *see* it, which was not at all the usual thing at night, but the sublime white light of the Savoy's electric chandeliers showed me everything in clear detail, gilded and moulded pillars and pediments and—and great urns with palm trees growing in them? Yes, palm trees growing indoors, displaying their fronds above low, plush armchairs larger than my bed, huge divans, and great burr-walnut cabinets bearing a treasury of shining things I could not identify, for I saw too much. Even though the space was immense, the crystalline illumination made everything seem to crowd in on me, overwhelming. It was not just because of my strait corset that I struggled to breathe.

Enola, this will not do.

Hiding my discombobulated face by languidly fanning myself, lifting my chin and also collecting myself mentally, I considered my mission: find that ruddy man, Rudyard Kipling. Where was he being feted? Certainly not on the ground floor, for such important events took place well away from the noise and dust of the street. My eyes turned to personages in full fig ascending the grandest staircase I had ever seen, and I had all but decided to follow them when I observed, farther across the huge and brilliantly lit room, a number of similar paragons of pulchritude forming a queue.

What in heaven's name? *There lived a sage in days of yore, and he a handsome pigtail wore,* I thought giddily, for I felt sure Thackeray could have written a witty poem about this queue, too. It was not at all an ordinary thing to see aristocrats condescending to stand in line. Curious to the bone, I had decided to join them even before it occurred to me that doing so was much to my advantage; my lack of an escort was unlikely to be noticed at such close quarters.

Taking as deep a breath as my corset would allow me, I instructed myself, *Ambulate like a ballerina, Enola.*

Deploy the toes outwards and glide. I let my luxurious fur slip down to show my bare shoulders, let my fan dangle from my wrist by its tasseled loop, fingered my jewelry (the hilt of my dagger) with my other hand, and sailed slowly across smooth seas—that is to say, the Savoy's gleaming marble floor. I felt a few curious glances catch upon me, and indeed I felt an utter fraud, but then, I reminded myself: exactly. Most of the people there, social climbers in shining raiment, were as much frauds as I was. Therefore, what did one more matter?

The end of the queue had somewhat unbraided itself so that, when I reached it, I was able to stand at the edge of a flock of females, as before. Like a woodcock (or perhaps a woodhen?) blending in, long bill and all, with its rustling, bustling forest, I hearkened to my surroundings.

". . . mere upstairs omnibus," intoned a man severely. "They'll never catch on."

". . . had a look at *Plain Tales from the Hills*," said another man who sounded terribly bored. "Purest bilge, you know, all mumbo-jumbo about India. . . ."

Somewhere near me, a woman whispered, "I rode a steam-powered one in New York last year, at Lord and Taylor's department store! Utterly thrilling!"

The severe man was saying, "Fine for lifting heavy, awkward things, masonry and such, but people?"

". . . chock full of the most exotic possible words," the bored man continued. "I believe him to be a bit too fond of the sound of his own voice."

". . . first time ever in an ascending room!" piped a female voice.

". . . the very latest . . ."

". . . phantom rickshaw . . ."

Would that the blazing white electric lamps could shed some illumination within my mind! I comprehended hardly anything, nor did it seem to make much sense that just a few hours ago, and less than a block away, I had seen what must have been, next to Jack the Ripper, the very most terrifying of urban bogeys: a mad dog. Once within the Savoy, I seemed to have passed into another world.

This sense of a wholly different reality continued when, along with the other people around me, I was ushered into a beautiful little carpeted room with a chandelier and mirrors and banquettes upholstered in velvet along the walls.

"Ladies, please be seated for safety," proclaimed a

glossily uniformed hotel official of some sort. "Please be seated for safety, all ladies." He stood beside a stout rope, indeed a cable, that ran from floor to ceiling—for what reason I could not imagine—but then I could, as "Now we shall ascend," he said, and with a portentous white-gloved hand he pulled a lever.

Having chosen not to consider myself a lady, I remained standing—quite buttressed in one place, for the room was crowded—and whilst at no time did my feet leave the floor, I felt the most peculiar uplifting sensation. Nor do I refer to any spiritual experience. It was quite physical; according to my innards, I was levitating. I was in the "ascending room," ye gods! Realizing that the room in its entirety was slowly, ever so slowly rising, with me in it, I am afraid I uttered something wordless and uncouth, but my embarrassment was minimal, for so did all the others.

"I say!" exclaimed nearly all the gentlemen in chorus.

Most of the women squeaked like kittens, then gasped, then started to chitter at one another. But just as some of them started to smile and become accustomed to being in this "upstairs omnibus," the white-gloved attendant once more applied himself to the lever, and the ascending room slowed, hesitated, then ceased to ascend.

"The hydraulic or steam-powered ones make a great deal more noise," the loudest male voice was saying.

"Quite marvelous, this vertical sort of electric vehicle," some other man answered.

And the mirrored wall I was facing simply slid away and disappeared, giving us egress to what seemed by comparison a vast Taj Mahal of a ballroom, all wreathed with peacock feathers, terribly brightly lit and equally brilliant with the sweet yet shrill notes of violins playing quite a come-hither sort of music, whilst upon the floor, flotillas of dancers swanned in the most exotic possible attitudes. "Tango! They're playing a tango!" whispered various excited voices around me. "All the rage in France!"

Whatever a tango was, it thrummed right through my entire personage. The crystalline light, the heartbeat of the music, the late hour, the thrill of adventure, the shock of wearing such a bare-shouldered disguise, the sight of so very many handsome men in white tie and tails—for whatever reasons, gliding forwards, I scarcely felt the assistance of my own feet. Again, I felt questioning eyes upon me, and I wondered whether my basted bertha was perhaps coming loose from my improvised dress, but mentally I shrugged my bare shoulders. So long as no one dared to stop me, it simply didn't matter.

"Champagne?" offered an exceedingly elegant maid carrying a tray of sparkling stemware.

"No, thank you," I murmured, "I don't seem to need it." To become tipsy would have been redundant. Peculiar India-themed decorations glittered all around me: sabres and ivory tusks arranged around green-and-orange cockades of ribbon on the oak-paneled walls, and various armaments nameless to me, and the head of a rhinoceros, and yet more taxidermy, including, on a pedestal and in its entirety, quite a large hooded cobra menacing to strike—and how in this delightful jungle was I supposed to find Ruddy? Whilst the women in their ball gowns flitted as various as butterflies, the men in their fancy dress appeared to me no more distinctive than so many magpies—if there were magpies in India.

I was not at all sure whether there were rhinoceroses in India either. Perhaps the quite odd-looking thing mounted on the wall was that of some other creature entirely. Perhaps a lumpen dragon of some sort.

I glanced hither and yon. The quite enchanting music, I discovered, issued from five doughty musicians—a string quartet and piano—elevated on a stage of sorts that was lavishly swagged with Indian-print draperies, but without curtains. They leaned into their instruments, the violins wept, the tango climaxed and, amidst the most extraordinary posturing of the dancers, ended. There was a muffled roar of impeccably gloved hands clapping. The musicians stood, bowed, and betook themselves away whilst a man of some official capacity—the butler of the ball?—mounted the platform.

"And now, honoured guests, ladies, gentlemen, nobility and peers of the realm," he bawled, "our most gracious patroness, Lady Sophronia, Marchioness of Sumatterbury!"

Because I remained in a kind of daze, I may spare the gentle reader any accounting of Lady Sophronia; I barely looked at her or listened to her. Passing, like the others, from the dance floor to an area of circular tables, twirling my fan, I was distracted by the fact that I trod on tiger-skin rugs, and the tables were topped by bowls of lotuses around ices shaped like elephants, some with howdahs, some not. I was wondering what it would be like to ride in a howdah, and, in a similar vein, whether or not I ought to settle in one of the low, soft chairs by the ivy-draped tables, when I noticed a crescendo rising in the Marchioness of Sumatterbury's voice: ". . . may I present to you the foremost literary figure of our time, the bard of India and poet of empire, Mr. Rudyard Kipling!"

I turned around, gawking, and there he was on the platform with his hands in his pockets and his head thrown back, looking rather a bully, although his voice (as he offered the conventional utterances of thanks and delight) sounded merely correct and querulous. Remembering the ill-tempered way he had laid hands on Joddy, I stopped listening to him, noticing only vaguely that he, the Ruddy man, proposed to recite one of his poems. I thought instead of how I might best accost him after he was finished speaking, and I turned my attention to possible paths of approach. Surely some roundabout and concealed route would be best. Taking note of the doors the servants used, I formed ideas of the passages that might exist behind the walls—

But such thoughts scarpered from my mind as a man's deepening voice, rhythmic and primeval, caught my ear.

"The Colonel's son has taken horse, and a raw rough dun was he, With the mouth of a bell and the heart of Hell and the head of a gallows-tree. . . ."

My heart quickened as if to tango, but this was a music made only of words. Standing straight as a spear in front of the piano on the dais, very still and staring at some distant wilderness far beyond the walls of the Savoy, the man, Rudyard Kipling, spoke on as if in a trance:

"The dun he leaned against the bit and slugged his head above, But the red mare played with the snaffle-bars, as a maiden plays with a glove. There was rock to the left and rock to the right, and low lean thorn be-tween, And thrice he heard a breech-bolt snick tho' never a man was seen."

I felt the danger, sensed the darkness, heard the galloping, galloping heartbeat cadence, and I remembered being called the she-demon Putana, and knew to my lanky bones that this Rudyard Kipling was a wizard with words.

"They have ridden the low moon out of the sky, their hoofs drum up the dawn, The dun he went like a wounded bull, but the mare like a new-roused fawn. The

dun he fell at a water-course—in a woeful heap fell he,
And Kamal has turned the red mare back, and pulled
the rider free. . . ."

Rapt, I listened to the rest of the poem about how
the two riders, enemies, stood face-to-face.

"'Twas only by favour of mine,' quoth he, 'ye rode so
long alive.'"

East was East, said Rudyard Kipling, and West was
West, and never the twain should meet, but when two
strong men faced each other and declared friendship,
East and West were no more. By the time he finished
chanting his poem, I longed to be like one of his heroes,
one of the two strong men pledged to be friends.

Evidently I was not the only one who felt so, for
the applause sounded like ten thousand grouse burst-
ing from cover all at once. Then the orchestra returned,
and intrepidly struck up a waltz, but only a few couples
danced. Seemingly three-quarters of the crowd ignored
the music, instead surging forwards to speak with Mr.
Kipling.

Necessarily, my errand being of the utmost impor-
tance, I included myself among that number.

Perhaps so as not to be trampled, Mr. Kipling remained

on the top of the steps that led up to the stage, speaking from there to the foremost of his many sycophants. "Thank you very much. Yes, I do truly believe in the austere love that binds men serving in Her Majesty's armed forces. . . ."

I heard him perfectly, as he spoke up to be heard above the music, and I noticed that his voice was no longer the deep, nuanced instrument of a poet; it was pitched higher now, with tones of petulant youth. After all, I realised, he was not much older than I.

"Yes," he said to the next sympathetic listener, "that's true, I did have a nervous breakdown, and I don't mind talking about it, for it was not at all my fault. It was completely due to unrequited love, you know. . . ."

Heavens, what a brazenly poetic word, "unrequited." No one ever spoke of "requited love," but this man quite possibly might. He was a glutton for oldish English. Or perhaps I should say oddish English.

To another man—naturally, the males had all pushed to the fore—in response to another man, he said, "No, nothing whatsoever have I heard, and Wolcott Balestier is my best friend—"

This was my opportunity for a word in his ear, yet I could not get anywhere near him, so in order to connect—I cannot otherwise sensibly explain it—I threw my fan at him. I can only say, in my defense, that, presented with a David and Goliath moment, I reacted appropriately. Like David, I whirled my only weapon and let fly with consummate accuracy. The painted-silk projectile struck Rudyard Kipling's starched and studded shirt-front, then fell to the floor.

There ensued quite a startled moment, during which he, and the crowd around him, stood mute and motionless whilst I hurried forwards, leading with my shoulder and plowing my way, gabbling inanities. "Oh dear so sorry my most abject blushes I do apologise cannot imagine how that happened it quite got away from me. . . ." The crowd hurriedly withdrew to let me pass whilst Ruddy, still speechless, bent over to pick up my fan. As he handed it back to me, I looked straight into his bespectacled eyes and told him, "I have news of Cotswold."

His eyes opened wide, and so did his mouth, but he said nothing.

"I need to speak with you," I said.

Still he just stood there gawking at me, not dealing at all competently with a perfectly simple situation.

Meanwhile, his sycophants began once more to clamour and crowd around him. "Mr. Kipling, when do you expect to finish your novel?" "Mr. Kipling, were you indeed brought up almost entirely in India?" "Mr. Kipling—" Failing to gain Ruddy's attention by vocal means, one member of the mob actually tugged at his sleeve. Next, I believed, they would grasp him by the arms and bear him away from me. Desperate measures were called for.

With an instant and heroic show of teeth, I acted. Beaming fit to outshine the electric illumination, I trilled, "Oh, Mr. Kipling, thank you! Yes, I would love to dance!"

Still ogling me and still wordless, nevertheless he stepped forwards and offered me his arm. Handing my fan and my fur wrap to a startled servant, I took Ruddy's elbow, and he escorted me to the dance floor. The gentle reader will kindly appreciate that I had never in my life danced, nor had I ever been instructed how to dance. However, I had been observing, and waltzing did not look difficult. One placed one's hands thus and so, then perambulated in circles. And surely, whilst doing so, one might speak privately to one's partner.

NANCY SPRINGER

"Daughter of a buffalo, who the hell are you?" burst out Mr. Rudyard Ruddy-rude Kipling before we had taken more than a few decorous steps.

Good. He did not recognise me as the ostrich biddy he had declared me to be; I had hoped he might not.

Archly I replied, "You should ask, rather, what I have learned of your friend. Perhaps, luxuriating within this palatial hotel, you are not aware that, a mere block away, a mad dog roams the streets?"

"Codswallop!" Vigorously halting me, he faced me, grasping me by both upper arms and glaring fit to be hydrophobic himself. "Are you trying to tell me there's such a thing here on the Strand in grand old London? Unmitigated hogwash!"

"Cotswold would beg to differ. The thing tore his leg open this past Thursday evening."

His face remained pugnacious, but I saw the colour drain out of it, and regretted having been so blunt. I did not think I had raised my voice as much as he had, but all around us heads turned and eyes fixed upon us. Abruptly, Ruddy released my arms and moved his hands so that one grasped mine, extending my arm like a horizontal flagpole, whilst the other pressed against my back, and he bodily swung me in a quarter circle, meanwhile performing a sort of gallumph.

Oh. The waltz. I dipped and swirled as best I could, taking note that our embarrassing proximity brought my mouth quite close to his ear, and of course one must take advantage of one's opportunities. "I have witnesses," I told him, exaggerating only slightly and keeping my voice quite quiet and level, "who saw the mad dog take hold of Wolcott Balestier's leg and bite him as he tried to subdue it with his stick."

"Then why did he not return home, or send word? It makes no sense!"

Being whirled around hither and yon, unable to think, I tried to deflect the question. "Was it not in character for him to intervene?"

Unfortunately, just at that point, the hem of my own dress got under my feet and tripped me. I staggered, losing my dance partner's hand, and he gave me a pointed, indeed piercing, look. With unmistakable sarcasm, he inquired, "Do you tango?" Blessedly, the waltz was slowing to a close. We stood still, but he kept speaking. "Who are you? *What* are you?" Abruptly he reached out and tugged at my improvised fancy collar, my bertha, which promptly and cheerfully parted company with my dress. "You're no lady! You're an impostor! A fraud!"

Oh, blast and damn. I blazed back at him, "I am Enola Holmes."

His bushy eyebrows shot up. Stepping back from me, he yelped, "You are that wild virago girl with the dagger!"

"Girl me no girl. I *shall* find your friend for you," I told him before turning my back, fetching my wrap, and making my exit (with a great many people staring at me, and with the best dignity I could muster) into the chilly springtime night.

Chapter the Sixth

Understandably, considering all I had been through, I slept until noon the next day, Sunday, thereby missing breakfast and elevenses. (The Professional Women's Club, with lodgers who were always on the go, served a business-like six meals a day: breakfast, elevenses, luncheon, tea, dinner, and supper. This arrangement suited me splendidly.) After luncheon, I returned to my neighbours the gloves, wrap, fan, jewelry, et cetera, I had borrowed, thanking them sincerely and laughing off their inquiries as to how my evening had gone. As for my "ball gown," in retrospect I fervidly desired to throw it on the fire, or—lacking a fire, for the ever-so-fickle weather had turned fine again—I wished to hurl it into the dustbin. Indeed, I was scowling at the sad vacancy the loss of two quite fashionable dresses had made in my wardrobe when there was a knock at my door.

The visitor was a maid who handed me a note which, upon opening, I discovered was from my brother. To say it was terse would be an understatement.

Enola I should like to see you at once Sherlock

I dismissed the maid, telling her no answer was required, and then, with perversity warming the cockles of my heart (whatever on earth a cockle might be!), I took the utmost time with my toilette. That is to say, I removed the dress I was wearing, sat in front of the mirror, and carefully applied recondite emollients to beautify my face, lips, eyelids, and eyelashes, and then at my leisure decided what might be my most fetching dress to wear. Dresses had changed a great deal in the brief few years I had been wearing them. Fashion had relinquished the bustle and its requisite draperies and overskirts in favour of greater simplicity below the waist but much more fuss above it. The delicately celadon-green frock I eventually donned had an elaborately tucked and pleated bodice, sleeves puffed at the shoulders, and a scalloped, starched collar almost two inches high. Not every woman could carry off the fashionably high neck, but I (ostrich biddy) could do so with flair. I donned my newest hat, an egg-shaped creation with the larger part of the brim in front and a jade-green froth of feathers in back. Avian millinery was quite the thing that spring of 1890, and many ladies wore hats adorned with doves, robins, bluebirds, and hedge-sparrows in their entirety—sometimes with wire-rigged, movable wings!—but I refused to go about with a dead bird on my head, settling for feathers instead. Making a mental note that I must, sometime soon, buy myself a new pair of gloves, green ones, to match my outfit, I put on my best yellow kid, selected a favourite parasol, and sallied forth.

At 221b Baker Street, I found my brother brooding over a problematic chessboard, nor did he rise when I entered the room. "Confound that Club of yours for not admitting men," he complained without looking at me, "I could have been and gone two hours ago."

"Why, Sherlock," I teased, "I thought you were inviting me for tea!"

He looked at me without quite raising his eyes heavenward, said "Ridiculous hat," and waved me to a seat across the table from him, as if I were to be his opponent at chess. From his waistcoat pocket he produced a folded paper I recognised as the note I had left him yesterday evening. He waved it at me in an annoying manner. "Enola," he demanded, "what is this nonsense about a mad dog?"

"It is not nonsense. I myself encountered the brute at close quarters. Only by climbing a sadly inadequate tree did I save myself."

He blinked, shook his head slightly, and went on, like a gramophone recording, without response. "I spent this entire morning gadding about London. No such dog has been reported to the police. No one in any of the hospitals knows anything about any victim of such a dog. And . . ." He leaned forwards, peering at me. "I have scoured Southwark. There is no Brosna Terrace and no Ethel Etheridge."

I am sure I looked quite blank. "But she was there," I insisted as if defending an ontological certainty, and immediately I produced paper and pencil from one of my pockets and began sketching her flat face, as if that alone would prove she existed. "She recognised my picture of Wolcott Balestier. She told me the mad dog had all but torn his leg off."

"What picture of Wolcott Balestier?"

"The one I drew." Completing a quick portrait of Ethel, or whatever her real name might be, I started another one of her remarkable profile.

"Enola," said Sherlock in an odd tone that caused me to glance up at him. The bridge of his nose had grown quite white, as if it were knuckles and his face was clenched. "Enola. My dear sister. You will please explain to me, here and now, how you came to be involved in this Balestier matter."

And, given time to marshal my thoughts, I would have done so, for his demand was not without reason. But as I drew breath and opened my mouth to begin, clamour interrupted me. Someone knocked with tremendous force on the downstairs door of 221 Baker Street. His attention startled away from me, Sherlock uttered a naughty exclamation, and both of us stood up as if we knew what might happen next. As it did.

Footsteps pounded up the stairs towards us, and Sherlock's door burst open.

"Mr. Holmes!" shouted a fraught male voice before we could even see who it was. "I have been informed of a most alarming possibility. A hydrophobic canine—"

But the instant he came in and caught sight of me standing by my brother, his words stopped, his feet likewise halted, and his jaw dropped. Otherwise, also, he was rather a mess; he wore neither hat nor gloves, and evidently had forgotten to comb his hair or shave. His skin formed dark crescents beneath his eyes—thus testifying to what late hours he kept—and he stood gawking.

Before he could stop gawking and speak, I ventured a step forwards and inclined my head courteously in his direction. "How do you do, Mr. Kipling?"

"You!" he yelped, glaring at me. "So help me, I'm hag-ridden by you, pestilent runnion, nothing more than a rag and a bone and a hank of hair! I wish you in perdition. Go—"

"Mr. Kipling," Sherlock interrupted smoothly, "I am sure you did not come here merely to anathematise my sister."

"Your *sister*!" Once more he stood with an apparently dislocated jaw, his mouth fumbling for air and words.

Graciously, and for the third time, I attempted to introduce myself. "Yes, I am his sister, Enola Holmes, Scientific Perditorian, finder of—"

But Sherlock interrupted me in my turn. "Enola, Mr. Kipling is *my* client, if you please."

"Beg pardon, I thought you worked for Miss Balestier." This was true. I turned to Mr. Kipling. "Knowing that this was officially my brother's affair, yesterday evening I reported my discovery concerning the mad dog first to him. However, when I found him not at home, I undertook to inform you—"

"By donning a ramshackle excuse for an evening gown and worming your way into my—" But in mid rant, Mr. Kipling caught sight of my drawings lying on the table and halted, staring, then pointing. "What is *she* doing here?"

Quick as a terrier, Sherlock asked, "Might you know her?"

"The platter-faced female who sells boutonnieres outside the Savoy."

"But do you know her name?"

"Why in all the halls of Jehovah should I?"

This time I spoke. "Because she is the one who saw the mad dog—"

She saw it attack Cotswold, I was going to say, but Sherlock interrupted, speaking in that pedantic way of his: "If she is not to be found, Enola, have you any other proof that Wolcott Balestier was bitten by a hydrophobic canid?"

"Just her, but I myself saw the dog, and she recognised a picture I had drawn of Cotswold—"

"A *picture* you drew!" yelped Kipling.

"My sister does excellent portraiture," Sherlock remarked.

Ruddy paid no heed. "Witnesses!" he bellowed. "Silly wench, you told me you had witnesses, in the plural!"

Sherlock said, "I beg you, my dear Mr. Kipling, to keep your head about you," and I protested, "I suspect the woman in the uniform of General Booth's Salvation Army knew something!" and at this point, gentle reader, it becomes difficult for me to recount the conversation sensibly, for all three of us spoke at once, with increasing heat, until Rudyard Kipling summed things up at the top of his lungs. ". . . the enormity of it!" he cried, his thick spectacles magnifying the wildness of his eyes. "Rabies? If so, he is sentenced to die a horrible, untimely death! I refuse so to despair!"

He hugged his head with his hands. "It's unthinkable! Surely there is a little time remaining to him, but where is he, and why has he not returned to his home, his sister?"

Sherlock said with finality, "I quite agree; the notion is unthinkable, by which I mean it lacks logic. There is no sense or evidence to support it." My brother gave me a curiously gentle glance, but went on all the same. "Mr. Kipling, please calm yourself. I feel certain you should simply put the idea of a rabid dog out of your mind. I myself intend to do so. Until we have more data, it seems to me that we should continue to pursue the more likely lines of inquiry."

I could not help but feel almost as if my brother had spanked me. But I maintained my composure admirably, and merely turned away, saying levelly enough, "I shall be going, then."

"You should be cursed," said a low, half-strangled voice—that of my brother's client.

"Mr. Kipling, *please*," Sherlock chided.

Snatching up my parasol, I walked briskly out of 221b Baker Street, down the stairs, and out the front door.

. . .

Due to a seething sensation in the region of my temper, I felt no inclination whatsoever to return home. I quite needed to treat and divert myself in some way. Moreover, I was wearing a quite fetching dress and hat, but had not yet received proper appreciation for them. While I did not know exactly what was the hour, which reminded me that I really ought to purchase a watch, I could see that the evening was young, because the sky was not yet dark. Accordingly, I marched the short distance to the Baker Street cabstand, where I engaged a hansom and directed the driver to take me to Drury Lane.

I had decided that, for once in my life, I was going to visit the Theatre Royal, denounced in pulpits throughout England because it provided entertainment on Sundays, and also scandalous and/or renowned for dramatic productions relying more on spectacle than on sense: carriage crashes including live horses onstage, a renowned flautist who played his instrument by using his posterior gasses, men of exotic origins performing sword dances, baby gi-raffes in a fashion parade, that sort of thing. As my cab let me out at one of the Ionic columns of the stately theatre building, and as I ambled at a fashionable pace towards the great entrance door, I wondered, attempting pleasant anticipation, what might await me on the programme this evening.

I was not to find out. "You!" cried a woman's voice. A whoosh of silk that sounded like a rising wind rushed up to me, and a dainty hand in a six-button calfskin opera glove seized my hand. My startled eyes looked down to discover Miss Caroline Balestier glaring up at me, her chin dangerously advanced. I saw, also, that a couple of her servants stood a respectful distance behind her, holding Cotswold's photographic portrait. She had been appealing to theatre-goers, then, before she spotted me.

"I know it was you who dressed up as a pauper," she declared in an accusing tone. *What did you think you were doing, spying in my house?"*

Much taken aback, I answered like a simpleton. "I was looking for your brother!"

"Up a chimney? Under a *bed*?" she retorted sarcastically.

This confrontation was not improving my already ill humour, but I held my temper because, wearing black as she was this evening, Miss Balestier looked almost as if she were in mourning.

Almost, but not quite. Her silk dress shone, whereas bombazine, the usual funereal fabric, admits of no luster—but I digress. "I wanted to discover something of Mr. Balestier's character," I told his sister earnestly. "His handwriting shows him to be most amiable. His stationery declares him to be an important man of letters. His—"

"Botheration! Just who the blue blazes do you think you are?" she interrupted most hotly and discourteously.

"Why not vermilion blazes, or heliotrope? And I *think* I am a perditorian, a finder of the lost," I retorted nearly as hotly. But then a dreadful thought chilled my fervor. Had Sherlock told her that he saw through my disguise? In a quite altered tone I besought, "Please, Miss Balestier, I beg you, tell me that Mr. Holmes did not betray me."

Some of her wrath gave way to puzzlement. "Not to me. I only overheard him telling my parlour-maid to be suspicious of paupers with all of their teeth, clean hair, and no dreadful odour of poverty," she said in a distracted way, but then her dark-eyed gaze hardened again and fixed on me. "Why do you mention him? Are you associated with him?"

"Hardly," I said, thinking bitterly of Sherlock's recent reprimand. And now this awkward encounter! During which the sun had gone; darkness now reigned, actually and metaphorically. I no longer had any desire whatsoever to be diverted and entertained by anything the Theatre Royal had to offer; I wished only to make a quick retreat, go home, and hide myself under a heap of blankets in my bed. "Miss Balestier," I addressed her with the best dignity I could muster, "I wish only to seek your brother and restore him to you. Finding the lost is what I do. Now, how can one more helper, myself, possibly harm you?" Then I turned and walked away.

"Wait!" she called after me. "Who are you? What is your name?"

I hastened my gait to a most unladylike stride, sprang into a waiting cab, and made my escape into the night.

• • •

Early, if not so very bright, the next morning I waited outside the tall double doorway of the Subscription Library in St. James's Square. Having spent a mostly sleepless night, and with small appetite for breakfast, I had arrived there before opening time, my carpetbag loaded with notebooks and pencils, my costume plain—a blouse, a skirt, and a straw boater, the simple garb of a scholar—and my mood, frankly, sour.

I had purchased a morning paper on my way to the library, to find headlined on the front page a shocked account of Wolcott Balestier's disappearance, with photograph (the selfsame photograph Ruddy had shown me), but with nary a mention of any mad dog.

Confound Sherlock for not believing me! How could he? But one must be fair, and making every effort to reason with myself, and acknowledging Sherlock's point of view as a professional detective with a dedication to data, I could somewhat understand why he had sided with his client against his own sister. However . . .

However, blessedly, the library opened its doors, admitting me into a cathedral-like atmosphere of learning. After consulting the card catalog (approving of a few newly typewritten cards among the many laboriously written in library hand), I located the topic of rabies, jotted down various Dewey numbers, and then, as if penetrating a dragon's cave, I quested into the formidable gridwork of intertwined, labyrinthine, cast-iron floors, ceilings, and bookshelves that comprised "the stacks."

Standing in one of the many narrow aisles constructed more like a railway crossing, able to see glimpses of people moving above my head and beneath my feet, I opened one book after another. I read: "The Metropolitan Streets Act was passed in 1867, enabling police to seize all vagrant dogs, and rabies thereafter declined . . . in 1887, twenty years later, a mere thirty persons in London died of rabies. . . ."

And now, in 1890, was it perhaps a mere twenty-five?

Of which Wolcott Balestier might become one.

"The onset of this horrid disease may begin as soon as two months, or as belatedly as six years, after the attack of the affected animal, and is therefore not always at first recognised as 'hydrophobia' or 'rabies,' but when that is, most misfortunately, the case, *it is invariably fatal.* Initially, the unfortunate victim may suffer only weakness, fever, headache and loss of appetite, but progression into the furious phase quickly follows. . . ."

Oh, dear. Inhaling a deep breath, I moved myself

and this particular book out of the stacks, to a "reading room" with tables (*not*, blessedly, made of cast iron) where I could sit down and take notes.

"... a typical case, the young female victim became excessively fatigued and complained of aches and shooting pains in her back. Anxious and melancholy, she appeared short of breath when trying to sip water. Within two days she found it quite impossible to eat or drink, and became confused and agitated to the point where she could not bear the touch of her own hair. Thereafter she was quite crazed with hallucinations, incontinent, and screaming with terror until she collapsed in a deep faint and, a week after she was first afflicted with this dreadful illness, she died without regaining consciousness."

Making a list of symptoms, my pencil had faltered to a halt in my hand. I closed my eyes, then opened them, staring at the nearest article of furniture, which happened to be a glass-fronted case filled with Chinese puzzle balls, globes within globes within globes of lacy "devil's work" carved from the ivory of long-expired mammoths.

For some moments I sat motionless, thinking of Cotswold, that gentle man, and what in the name of all horrors might be happening to him? He was bitten Thursday evening; already it was now Monday; could he already have fallen ill? Could he possibly be already deceased of the dreadful disease? No, no, surely not—but even if I could manage to locate him, he would still be doomed to succumb later if not sooner, amidst horrific suffering. Perhaps he was absenting himself for that very reason, to spare his sister! If so, how was I to find him? And for what purpose? How, in the name of all mercy, was he to be saved from rabies?

There had to be a way out of his dreadful fate. I had heard of someone . . . vaguely, over the past few years, I'd heard news of a scientist in France. . . .

Scooping up notebook and pencil, I arose and sought out the "reference" section of the library, where ponderous tomes did not circulate but sat like sages on the shelves, and where "reference librarians" seemed to know everything that was to be found in them. Tracking down such a librarian—a thin and elderly man who resembled a trout fly, for he was bent over and his downy hair trailed like feathers—to this remarkable person I spoke, or rather, in the hush of the surroundings, I whispered. He nodded, shuffled away, and eventually returned bearing some formidable-looking medical journals he placed on a table before me. Somewhat at a loss, for they were written in almost incomprehensible scientific terminology, I opened them one after another to pages I found marked with slips of paper, and eventually, with rising excitement, I was able to gather the following:

Louis Pasteur, scientist. Paris, France. 1885—five years ago. By doing something with the spinal cord of a rabbit that had died from rabies, this Pasteur gentleman had saved the life of a nine-year-old boy who had been torn open in fourteen places by a huge mad dog. How, exactly, he had gone about accomplishing this feat was not at all clear to me, but the process was called "inoculation."

I had never heard of such a procedure. It seemed quite far-fetched. Nevertheless, Wolcott Balestier, who moved in exalted literary circles, might have heard wondrous things of it. Could he possibly be fleeing from London to Paris in search of Pasteur?

I had to find out more.

With a nod of thanks to the hook-shaped gentleman, and quitting the library, I hailed a cab to take me
to another font of information, the mansion where a val-
etudinarian never ventured out of her third-storey bedroom, yet knew everyone and heard everything: Florence
Nightingale.

Chapter the Seventh

I had first met Florence Nightingale whilst investigating the disappearance of my sweet old landlady, who had been seized by ruffians who wanted to know about some message to "the Bird"—a Nightingale, perhaps. I had been astonished to find the heroine of the Crimean War yet alive, and even more astonished to find that she all but ruled England from her bed, even though she strictly secluded herself from the world below. Yet she had helped me find Mrs. Tupper, and she had become a rather good friend of mine.

"I allow this only because I want to have a look at

you," she remarked as I entered her airy eyrie at the top of her Hyde Park house, her bedroom/office/refuge where not even the Prime Minister was welcome to enter. "My, my," she marveled as I circumnavigated her bed to get to the one and only chair, "you certainly do maintain a variety of appearances. A scholar today, are you?" Propped up on pillows, their white linens decorated with embroidered flowers, she watched me as if enjoying a parade.

"Most days," I told her, although, truth be told, this Wolcott Balestier business had made me forget all about my studies.

"Studies? You, Enola? It seems only yesterday when I saw you leap out of this window to swing away through the trees with all the dexterity of a monkey, remarkable creature that you are."

Seating myself beneath that well-remembered window by her bed, I had to smile. "That was a good while ago."

"Yes." Her hair had gone white since then, but lay smooth as ever, parted in the exact center and flanking her placid face like shining wings. "But all is well now between you and your brothers?"

Blast, she had made me think of Sherlock, and the thought stung. Instead of answering, I gestured vaguely and urgently leaned towards her. "Please, Miss Nightingale, did you see the news of Wolcott Balestier's disappearance in today's papers?"

"Is *that* what brings you here."

"Yes. I have learned he was bitten by a mad dog—"

Her eyes widened. "There is no mention of that in the newspapers."

I admit I made an impatient gesture. "People seem not to believe me. But imagine, please, if you will, an educated man who finds himself suddenly and horribly afflicted with the—not actually rabies, yet, but the dread of rabies. Perhaps because of such dread, he has not returned home. But where in London might he go?"

"Surely to a medical man or some hospital?"

"All have been canvassed with no happy result. Is there any place particularly known for rabies?"

"Like a leper colony for latent hydrophobics?" she murmured, her eyebrows uncertainly poised. For quite a while she thought before she answered slowly, "I know of no such place. There is a government commission charged with rabies investigations, and it is headed by, I believe, a surgeon named Lister. Lord Joseph Lister. But I cannot imagine how he could possibly be involved."

Nor could I. Nor, with Florence Nightingale, was there any need to linger politely and speak of nothing. We each knew the other desired no ceremonial kisses and had much to do. With thanks, I took my leave.

Thanks for what? I mused, scowling, the moment I closed the door behind me. Florence Nightingale had been of very little help. How was I ever to find Wolcott Balestier? I gave this problem useless and despairing thoughts as I descended the stairs to visit with Mrs. Tupper, my former landlady. I did not feel particularly amiable, but Mrs. Tupper was sure to know I was in the house, and she would be hurt if I did not pay her a visit.

Mrs. Tupper, tiny, deaf, a survivor of the Crimean War, was living out her final days in the home of Florence Nightingale, so arranged by a combination of that lady's hospitality and my reimbursing her for the expense involved. I found Mrs. Tupper, as usual, sitting right beside the grand piano in the recital room, close enough to somewhat hear, or sense, the music if anyone should start to play the instrument. When I walked in, she greeted me with an inarticulate cry of pleasure, and, after giving her a hug, I pulled up another chair to sit beside her, then produced pencil and paper from my carpetbag.

You see, it was nearly impossible to have a normal conversation with her anymore, her deafness had grown so dire. Instead of shouting at her, on paper I printed in large coarse-hand letters a few conventional inquiries about her health and well-being, which she answered loquaciously. "What are you doing these days?" she shouted at me as if I were the deaf one. By way of answer, I vigorously drew a picture of the mad dog rampaging, froth of saliva dripping from its snarling fangs. Mrs. Tupper gasped, both twiggy hands flying to her mouth. Hastily I added to the background a sketch of myself safe in a tree.

"Thank God yer not bit!" exclaimed Mrs. Tupper. "You seen a mad dog in the street?"

I nodded.

She leaned towards me, placing one withered hand on my arm. "I remember the first time I seed one, when I were a child, how dreadful it were. My mama picked me up and run away, but I seed it over her shoulder. It come, a big yeller dog it was, the mad dog come down our street roaring and raging and foaming at the mouth and eyes like live coals. . . ."

Mrs. Tupper described the dog and its fearsome antics at length, and detailed so thoroughly how people screamed and fled, that my attention began to wane. I remember only vaguely how she spoke of a few brave neighbourhood men who rallied to arm themselves and attack the menace.

". . . knocked the dog down at last and killed it with their cudgels," she concluded, "but not before it caught a feller, pulled him down, and mauled him. The neighbours, even the women, my own mother among them, they picked up bricks and stones and such and set on that man and killed him right then and there, so they did, before he could become a deadly danger to them."

My jaw dropped, and so did my pencil, slipping from my slackened fingers and falling to the parquet floor.

"With cudgels an' sticks an' axes and such, too," Mrs. Tupper loudly explained in response to my shock. "Killed the dog first, of course, but didn't wait no time before they turned on the feller what got bit. They knowed good and proper that it were either him or contagion, you see, no two ways about it, so they put him to death just like they done the dog."

"Oh, my stars and garters," I murmured, shaken by thoughts so disconcerting I completely disregarded the loss of my pencil.

"And took them both away to bury them deep. The dog as far away as they could, you know, but the feller what got bit, they laid him to rest more decent-like, in the churchyard and all, with sorrow, but they buried him extra deep just the same."

"Oh, my dear brother Sherlock," I muttered, remembering how my brother had scoffed at any possibility that a man bitten by a rabid dog might not immediately return home.

But—could it be? Could it possibly still be happening in this more enlightened day? Was what I was thinking even thinkable?

Nevertheless, think it I did, and the thought drove me to my feet quite abruptly. "Good-bye for now," I told Mrs. Tupper, bending to hug her around her skinny shoulders and kiss her shriveled cheek. I then, blessedly, remembered to retrieve my lost pencil and seize my carpetbag.

"But where are ye going?" quavered Mrs. Tupper.

"To Covent Garden Flower Market!" I bellowed into the trumpet she held to her ear.

• • •

I quite needed to talk once again to the boutonniere vendor whose name was not Ethel Etheridge, and because that was not her name, I could not inquire after her by any conventional means.

As Rudyard Kipling was no longer being feted at the Savoy, and therefore she no longer had any occasion to sell boutonnieres there, I had to locate her elsewhere. I needed to track her down.

And how better than by her wares? Her flowers. And where else would she supply herself with fresh carnations, cornflowers, and gardenias except the enormous open-air market at Covent Garden?

But, poised in the doorway of my cab to alight there, scanning chaotic, crowded acres of carts, stalls, bargainers, and cut flowers, I boggled at the task I had set myself. It could take days for me to find the flat-faced woman I sought, and meanwhile what might be happening to a young gentleman with a puckish smile and winsome eyes? He might not have so many days!

I stepped down from the cab, paid the driver, and walked into the market amidst throngs of people and billows of peonies, pink roses, lilacs, and lilies, their beauty and blended scents almost fit to drown in. I shook my head against their lure, telling myself, *Think*.

I thought. From the point of view of a boutonniere seller. Then I diverged from peonies, pink roses, lilacs, et cetera, and headed in a different direction. But before I reached the area of the flower market that I was headed for, amidst the many voices babbling all around me I thought I heard . . .

I hearkened, my mouth slightly ajar with surprise. Yes, indeed, I heard a very familiar voice crisply questioning a nearby vendor, "Might you identify this woman?"

I turned, and there was my brother Sherlock, top hat and all, showing the vendor something of *mine*—the picture I had been so careless as to leave in his flat, that of the flat-faced woman whose name was not Ethel Etheridge.

The vendor was answering Sherlock in the negative when I strode over, tapped my brother not at all timidly on his shoulder, and told him to his startled face, "You are looking in the wrong area."

"Enola!" he blurted, his expression of temporary stupidity most gratifying.

I continued, "Society dictates that boutonnieres shall be made only of red or white carnations, blue cornflowers, or white gardenias. You will not find those, or the woman you are hunting—" Rather fiercely I snatched my drawing away from him and thrust it into my carpetbag where it belonged. "You will not find anything of use here amidst the damask roses."

"Enola," he expostulated, "if you will listen for a moment—"

I countered his frown with my own. "Moreover," I lectured, "a vendor of boutonnieres would most likely purchase her blossoms in the thriftiest of all possible ways, namely from yesterday's batches of flowers, of which she need choose only the fresher specimens and throw the rest away. You will find 'seconds' at the far end of the market—"

"Enola," he rudely interrupted, "what are you doing here?"

"The same thing you are doing!" But then astonishment trumped my vexation. I gawked at him. "You expected I would go home and give up?"

Just for an instant he looked uncomfortable, even perhaps a trifle guilty, which mollified me.

"Didn't you?" I challenged more quietly.

"I thought you were angry," he said quite softly. "Regrettable, but dismissing you seemed necessary at the time."

"Why?"

"To placate my client."

I made a face at the mention of Mr. Kipling, but suddenly I quite understood. The client came first. Of course.

"However, as you can see by catching me here, I have not completely discarded your rabid-dog theory," Sherlock added. "One must tie up the loose ends."

"But it's not a loose end!" I cried, and I am sure distress showed in my face as I thought of what Mrs. Tupper had said. "It's getting tighter by the moment, and snapping like a whip! Sherlock, there is something I need to tell you."

His eyebrows rose sharply. "Then let us adjourn to

less crowded quarters," he said, taking me by the elbow and steering me out of the flower market.

. . .

Both of my brothers can be remarkably obtuse, for brilliantly intelligent men, when it comes to democratic modes of transportation. Neither would ever set foot in an underground railway, and when Sherlock traveled by train, it was never, ever in a third-class carriage. In this instance, an omnibus paused at a Covent Garden kerb, but Sherlock would have nothing to do with it. So, as no cabs were available, we set off towards the nearest tea room on foot. Sherlock offered his arm, and we proceeded in silence, our attention fully taken up by the exigencies of navigating the crowded streets.

Certainly one saw all kinds. We made our way amongst women pushing perambulators, ladies with parasols, a fellow with a wooden leg helping another fellow with crutches, humble clerks and artisans, and far less humble military men, gents, swells, and toffs. I ignored them and a girl selling tussie-mussies. No matter how great the stench, I have never been one to hold flowers to my nose, even though to do so would have helped to conceal its unlovely length. But not so, I saw, a stout woman on the other side of the street, wearing a blue serge uniform; the ebullient nosegay she held to her face contrasted strangely with her stern, old-fashioned black straw bonnet—

I gasped, let go of Sherlock's arm, dropped my carpetbag at his feet, and dashed towards her, leaving my brother in my dust, risking life and limb to dart between carts, coaches, and cabs, for I recognised her. Even though her posy hid her alarming chin, I still knew her to be the "Hallelujah Lassie" with whom I had spoken two nights ago. She had warned me against a large Alsatian dog roaming the area of the Strand. And something in her manner had suggested she knew somewhat more about that dog than she had spoken.

"Excuse me!" I cried as I reached her side, panting. She turned her very startled face towards me.

"You saw!" I cried, almost imploring. "You *saw* that mad dog attack, didn't you?"

To my astonishment—for Salvation Army minions are reputed to be the gentlest of spiritual warriors—to my utter disbelief, she instantly, quick as a terrier, hurled her posy hard into my face—and she fled! She hoisted her skirt and sprinted away. But I had to clear pansies away from my eyes before I could hoist mine and run after her.

I had quite enjoyed running in my younger years when I wore knickerbockers, hand-me-downs from my older brothers. But in a skirt—! I quite wished to yell something naughty, for I found it most annoying to have to deal with my skirt, arms so awkwardly positioned forwards to hold it up, rather than pumping by my sides. Still, wobbling along like a great goose, I managed to lessen the distance between myself and my prey—until she looked back, saw me closing in, and toppled a stack of bushel baskets directly across my path. Circumnavigating these, I saw with alarm that she was making towards the market, in which labyrinth of chaos she could easily lose me. Blast it, I quite wanted a speedy mount of some sort, a bicycle or even a horse, for four legs are faster than two, but all equines near at hand were inimically harnessed to vehicles. However, a herd of beef still on the hoof chanced to be bellowing past, so I leapt to seat myself on the nearest steer, a harlequin-spotted creature.

Giving him no time to protest, I seized his ears, pointed his snout in the direction of my fleeing prey, and kicked him smartly in the ribs.

Nor, might I remark, did I ride him sidesaddle. Quite the opposite. My skirt shockingly pushed up so far—dare I say it!—so far as to expose my knees, I rode him blatantly astride. Otherwise—as I well knew, having occasionally, in my free-and-easy childhood days, tried to ride sheep—otherwise, I would not have been able to hang on in the only possible way, by clinging with my lower limbs. As I expected, the steer flung himself upwards and forwards in such a feckless and impetuous manner that I had a hard time aiming him towards my selected screaming and fleeing female (among many other pedestrians who were now screaming and fleeing) but I did succeed—up to a point. We (the steer and I) had just caught up with her when, with a tremendous buck, he dislodged me and sent me flying.

Luckily, I sailed right into her, knocking her over and landing on top of her.

She fell flat on the pavement, whereas I merely fell on top of her, a far lesser impact. She moaned, poor soul, and showed small resistance as I rolled her over onto her back and pinned her by her upper arms. However, I could see she was not much injured, for her close-set eyes looked thoroughly alive. Indeed, wide open, they looked nearly ready to jump out of her flushed face.

"This Thursday evening past," I enunciated, my face inches from hers, "on the Strand, a rabid raving mad black Alsatian attacked a gentleman. You saw."

No words came out of her slack-jawed mouth.

"You *saw!*" I shook her as if to awaken her. "What happened to the man who was bitten?"

She blurted, "I, I, um, I don't know nothing except they took him."

This revelation shook me so much that I let go of her. "Took him? Who?"

"They, um, the brethren of the street!"

A rough, unmistakably masculine grip seized me by the shoulder and yanked me to my feet. "See here!" roared a man's fraught voice in my ear. "Whatcher mean interferin' with my cattle!"

At the same time a tall gentleman stepped past me and bent over my victim to offer assistance. "What an unfortunate accident!" he said in almost hypnotically soothing tones. "Or possibly a random act of sheerest monomaniacal lunacy?" It was, of course, my brother Sherlock. With one impeccably kid-gloved hand he helped the unfortunate woman to arise; with the other he offered money to the shouting cattle-driver. The latter ceased his clamour and let go of me to accept the bribe, my victim stood straightening her black straw bonnet and her very plain navy-blue dress; both of their backs were turned away from me, and Sherlock mouthed at me, "Vanish."

I did so at once, and not without appropriate gratitude. Retreating, I heard my brother ask the much-abused woman with his most fulsome sympathy, "Whatever possessed that strange young female? What was she saying? Something about a mad dog?"

Concealing myself behind a wagon loaded with rhubarb and purple broccoli, whilst the angry man drove his steers away I peeked between bushel baskets of this interesting produce, watching Sherlock most solicitously converse with the woman he had just "rescued." I have seldom seen him act more charming, and she seemed to confide in him completely. At one point he showed her something—a card, a photograph? At another point he produced a small notebook from his breast pocket and wrote in it. Eventually he bowed, tipping his top hat to her, and they parted. She hurried on her way, and he strolled blandly on his, stopping to purchase a newspaper and scan its headlines.

When the Hallelujah Lassie had disappeared in the crowd, I joined my brother behind the newspaper. He looked me up and down, his face carefully expressionless. I was, I realised, a mess. I had lost my hat, my maidenly tresses had straggled loose from their chignon, the perspiration and hair of my erstwhile mount quite encrusted my clothing, and I smelled like a barnyard.

Without a hint of censure, my brother said, "Enola, words quite fail me."

I said, "Kindly let them continue to fail you in that regard. Do you now believe that there was a mad dog, that Wolcott Balestier was bitten by it, and that something even more fearsome may have happened to him?"

He stood there in a brown study—that is to say, staring aimlessly into the air of London, which was indeed brown or blackish most days—and it took him a moment to focus on me and answer, "It is not a matter of belief. I need data, Enola."

"And did that woman not give you data?"

"Her name is Agatha Bellwether. She confirmed that there was a mad dog near the Savoy this past Thursday, and that a gentleman was bitten by it. I showed her a photograph of Balestier, and she identified him as the gentleman. Where he is now, she seems to have no idea. Because she has taken an oath of honesty in order to join the organization whose uniform she wears, I am inclined to believe her."

"Are you also, now, more inclined to believe me?"

"I must admit I am. As we cannot possibly go to a tea room with you in such a state, would you like to tell me, here and now, what is on your mind?"

Perhaps because I had scared away half the populace, the street was quiet enough. I nodded. "I have been talking with Mrs. Tupper." Something seemed to constrict around my heart, and my voice quivered. "She said that, when she was a child, she saw her mother and some other neighbouring people beat a man to death. They killed him on the spot because he had been bitten by a mad dog."

Chapter the Eighth

Sherlock had very little to say after that. He hailed me a cab—not a hansom, in consideration of my disheveled state, but a closed cab, a growler—and after he had paid for it, as he handed me into it, he admitted, "I must at once go to inform my client about this grim turn of affairs."

"Your client came to me first." Why could I suddenly tell Sherlock about this now? Perhaps because words had failed him a few minutes ago? "Before he retained *you*, Rudyard Kipling came looking for Dr. Ragostin, and was quite rude to me when I offered to find Wolcott Balestier for him."

His face lighted up, and he gave a soft whistle of comprehension. "So therefore, of course, you are determined to do so!"

"Yes," I admitted. "Also, I have begun to care about Cotswold."

"As does Mr. Kipling, very much. Enola," said Sherlock with a change of tone, "please do not think too badly of Kipling. He is a very troubled man. Fame is not a comfortable thing, you know." He lowered his eyes, gave a nod, and began to turn away, his cheeks a bit pink, to my astonishment—I had never before seen him show the least sign of bashfulness.

"Sherlock, wait! My carpetbag!" I would have asked for my hat, too, but we had already seen it lying squashed in the street.

Sherlock made a complicated gesture of frustration and assent, said, "Wait; I'll just be a moment," to the cab-driver, and hurried off on my errand.

The moment my brother's back was turned, I stood up with my head and shoulders outside and hissed, "Driver!"

122

He turned his face, which was rather like that of a pug dog, towards me.

In the recent scuffle, my blouse had lost some buttons, enabling me, despite my high collar, to reach into my corset and bring forth money, substantial money, which I exhibited to him. "We *shall* go where that man has told you, but not just yet," I ordered him, gazing straight at his button-like eyes in his heavily jowled face. "First, taking every care not to be seen by him, we will follow him to discover where *he* goes." Chances were that my brother was going to speak with his client, and I quite wanted to find out where Rudyard Kipling lived; surely the knowledge would become useful to me. "For doing this, and doing it well, I will pay you handsomely."

He only stared at me.

"Do you agree?" I pressed him.

He continued to look back at me without answering. Then, instead of saying yes or no, he demanded, "Be you 'Arry's Miss Enoler?"

This was most unexpected. For a moment I did not understand, and then I realised he was referring to Harold. I am sure my jaw dropped, and I didn't know what to say.

He repeated, "Be you 'Arry's Miss Enoler?"

I managed to make my mouth function. "Yes," I whispered.

"Aw right, then." He turned away, and I shoved myself back inside the cab, seating myself in a hurry before Sherlock returned, and feeling a bit shocked. I, also, appeared to have notoriety of a sort, if only among cabdrivers. And Sherlock was right; it did not feel entirely comfortable. Suddenly I realised why my brother had shied away: speaking of fame, he had been speaking, in part, of himself.

He reappeared with my carpetbag, which looked none the worse for wear, and as he stood once more at the cab door to deliver it, he asked, "Shall you continue searching for the woman who was selling boutonnieres?"

"Yes."

"As shall I." Departing, he gave me a nod that was almost the sketch of a bow.

I felt, I must admit, a distinct glow. All was well between me and Sherlock. All was very good indeed. Despite the fact that I was going to spy on him.

As for that, my cabbie made a clever job of it, circling

the block and then waiting for my brother to pass (quite clearly it was he, Sherlock, plain to see in a hansom) before joining traffic some slight distance behind him. The drive was slow due to the usual vagaries of London traffic (carriage wheels locked together, various fist-fights, a misunderstanding between a tandem team of draft horses and a yoke of oxen, a lady knocked over at a crossing and having the vapours); therefore, it was easy to keep the hansom in sight all the way to its destination, which turned out to be 43 Villiers Street, Charing Cross, London. Kipling lodged not far from the Embankment and directly across from a music hall!

The cab-driver (whose name was Bert; I asked him when I paid him, and thanked him) then took me home to the Professional Women's Club, where I spent the afternoon, after ordering a luncheon tray, in close consultation with a bath-tub and my wardrobe, effecting a complete refurbishing of my personage.

Clad quite nicely, then, in an evening visiting costume of blue silk and dotted swiss, a be-feathered blue hat to match, and four-button gloves—that is to say, emboldened by my impeccable outfit, and after some girding up of mental loins, I sallied forth to call on Dr. Watson at home.

With, I might add, my carpetbag in hand.

• • •

Luckily, both the good doctor and his wife were in and welcomed me warmly, hiding their surprise at my unexpected arrival. Mrs. Watson kissed me and said, "Why, hello, Miss Viola Everseau!" such being the guise in which I had first met her. Watson came into the parlour from his surgery—he had, I thought, gained a little bit of weight since I had last seen him, but not too much—and he headed straight for a plate of macaroons, helping himself to several before he sat down across from me. Handing me a glass of lemonade and him a glass of something slightly stronger, Mary Watson joined us.

"By my oath, this is a treat!" said Watson, beaming. "It's been nothing but dropsy-pleurisy-quinsy day until you appeared."

"I might not prove to be much relief," I demurred, feeling genuinely apologetic. "I've come to delve your medical knowledge."

"Such as it is, you're welcome to all you like!" he responded, smiling, if possible, even more widely.

"I find myself woefully ignorant of rabies."

That single word, "rabies," quite stopped Watson's smile. He almost looked angry. No, it was not exactly anger I saw on his face. . . . I did not understand—

But his wife did, saying tenderly, "You have had patients die of rabies, haven't you, dear?"

"Certainly. If they have rabies, they always die. It's enough to—" But he halted without saying what it was enough to do. "It is a cruel way to die," he continued in a very low tone, "cruel for the victim, cruel for the family. One wants to help, but one cannot, one does not dare. Once they start to rave, even their nearest and dearest cannot comfort them. They attack and bite anything— the bedposts, the washstand, chairs, candlesticks, their loved ones—all with equal savagery. They must be restrained, tied down, bound head and hand and foot, to keep them from passing the contagion to everyone around them. As a doctor, one wants to *care* for them—" He broke off for a moment, looking at me as if to search for understanding. "One wants to ease their distress somehow, soothe them, make them comfortable, at the very least clean them when they soil themselves—but the sight of a basin of bath water makes them shriek and recoil in terror. One wants to wipe the everlasting froth from their faces. . . ."

Quite suddenly Dr. Watson ceased speaking and turned away.

After a little silence, "There is a reason it's called hydrophobia," his wife said gently.

Watson nodded, grimaced, then said, "They cannot seem to swallow. They drool at the mouth and seem to be choking, yet should one offer them a drink of water, they react as if one is threatening them with torture." His hands, in his lap, had clenched into fists, and I think he noticed this, for he took a deep breath, relaxed his hands, placed them on the arms of his chair, then raised his eyebrows at me. "Enola, I almost fear to ask—what on earth leads you to inquire about this frightful disease?"

I sighed, then answered as simply as I could. "A young man is missing. I've been told he was bitten by a rabid dog. Almost a week ago." I leaned towards the doctor in appeal. "Might he yet be alive?"

Watson at once resumed his professional manner,

sitting back and stroking his moustache. "Was this man in normal health, otherwise?"

"As far as I know, yes."

"Upon what part of his body was he bitten?"

"In the leg."

"Lower leg?"

"I think so, yes."

Dr. Watson rearranged himself, fingertips together and pointed upwards like a church steeple, to hold forth. "Quaintly enough, the prognosis of this wretched disease seems to depend on the location on the body of the bite. Enola, if your young man had been mauled all over the body, or bitten on the face, the prospect would be much grimmer. But if only on the lower extremity, I can say with some assurance that it will take the mania months, perhaps even years, to worm its way to his brain."

"Then there might still be time to do—something. If I can find him."

"Do something?" Watson stared at me. "What can possibly be done?"

"Isn't there some treatment recently discovered?"

"Treatment?"

"By a scientist in France, I think it was. . . ." But I

could not clearly remember anything I had read in the library that morning, which felt as if it were eons ago. "Wait. I wrote it down." Reaching down into my carpetbag, I rummaged for my notebooks, impatiently pulling out the papers that got in my way and tossing them aside—

Dr. Watson exclaimed, "What are you doing with a picture of Mary Erasmus?"

I looked up to find him staring at my sketch of the flat-faced woman who sold boutonnieres.

I gasped. "You know her?"

"She has been a patient of mine."

"What is her name again?" I demanded, pencil poised to write it down.

"Mary Erasmus." Dr. Watson seemed a bit embarrassed for some reason. "But I do not know her well. Her name stuck in my mind because it made me think of marasmus. A medical term," he then explained, due to my blank look, "meaning emaciation or extreme malnourishment. It struck me as being almost comically, ah, inappropriate at the time."

From this I deduced that he had noticed how plump

Mary Erasmus was beneath the restraint of her corset. I smiled. "Where does she live?"

"That I do not know. I have seen her only in the office, for boringly ordinary complaints. Who is she?"

"A witness. One of two witnesses I have found so far." Another thought occurred to me. "Dr. Watson, have you ever heard of a group called 'the brethren of the streets'?"

He had not, nor had his wife, and the conversation strayed elsewhere; I had not the heart to bring up the subject of rabies again. As soon as I felt I decently could, with many thanks and much affection I departed. What had been a sunny springtime day had turned to chilly darkness by the time I arrived back at the Professional Women's Club, and I quite wanted my supper, but first I had an important note to write.

Dear Sherlock,
Miss (or perhaps Mrs.) Mary Erasmus is
the boutonniere vendor's actual name. I have this
on good authority. How to trace her? I think she
is an educated woman. She exhibited remarkable
vocabulary when I spoke with her.

Please inform, have the police yet anything re Wolcott Balestier or the mad dog that attacked him?

Sincerely,
Enola

I posted this after supper but before I went to bed.

· · ·

The next morning, Tuesday, I made myself get up, wash my face, put on a nice frock, and altogether become civilised in time to join the other Professional Women downstairs in the dining room for breakfast, all for the sake of some gossip. After serving myself at the sideboard, avoiding the deviled kidneys but partaking of some oysters, head cheese, and hot buns, I sat at table, sipped a cup of strong, black tea, and joined in the matutinal chatter.

Several voices greeted me, "Enola! How goes the sleuthing?" or similar inquiries, and I gave slight answers and asked in my turn how they were doing with their Suffragist activities, their medical studies, their music students, their experiments in typewritten art, their tutoring, and their other efforts to keep the wolf from the door. Once the conversation had slowed a bit, I managed to steer it towards reading, and asked of everyone in general, "Do you like Kipling?"

"I don't know, I've never kippled!" returned several in unison, giggling.

"What is there to like?" demanded one of the older women, a telegraph operator. "All he writes is doggerel about the great British soldier brutalizing India."

"No, that is not all he writes," protested my neighbour the equine phrenologist. "Some of his poetry is actually quite good, and I have heard he is working on a novel, his first."

"It is said to be about an artist," agreed an authoritative woman who worked on Fleet Street. "Apparently Kipling is attempting quite a serious work about a gifted young painter who goes blind."

"How very tragic!" responded the telegraph operator with good-natured sarcasm. "So, are you saying he is capable of more sympathetic literature?"

"Perhaps. His novel-in-progress is said to be also a story of unrequited love."

"Yes, really, one must not hold it against the man

that he was born male," yet another woman put in. "Behind his scowl, you know, Kipling is really a sensitive soul. Why, he recently suffered a nervous breakdown."

"Really!" several listeners chorused.

"Yes, he is just recovering, largely thanks to the influence of his new literary agent, one Wolcott Balestier, a charming American gentleman of the very finest sensibilities."

"American!" exclaimed several ladies at once, and the sarcastic telegraph operator added, "With *sensibilities?*"

"It is possible, you know," said the Fleet Street woman. "Kipling and young Balestier are said to be bosom good friends, fine old-fashioned loving comrades, and partners in the writing business."

So emphatic was her tone that the subject was considered closed, and no one, I noticed, had mentioned that Wolcott Balestier had gone missing. As the talk switched over to the Madhist War going on in the Sudan, I finished eating and excused myself, wandering off to decide what best to do.

I quite wanted to tell the Fleet Street woman all about Wolcott Balestier, but knew I had better not.

Publicity might well be helpful, but that was a matter to be determined by Sherlock and his client.

Should I return to the Covent Garden Flower Market to search for the flat-faced woman whose name I now knew—Mary Erasmus? But Sherlock was seeking the same person, and he had Scotland Yard connexions, so any efforts on my part might be a waste of time. For Wolcott Balestier's sake, I could not afford to waste any time.

How to proceed?

Hmmm.

Chapter the Ninth

Not much more than an hour later, having changed out of my nice frock into a much humbler one, wearing my oldest boots, very shabby white cotton gloves, and a scarf tied over my head (having lost my boater), I sallied forth.

Harold, waiting for me atop his cab, greeted me, "Good morning, Miss Enola," with an inquisitive look. As often happened, he brought forth the imp in me, because, while he obviously took an interest in my escapades, propriety forbade him to ask questions.

So I answered him only with a mischievous smile.

"Good morning, Harold. Let us go first to Finchwhistle Terrace."

There I called on my good friends, twin sisters Tish and Flossie Glover, who occupied adjoining flats on the top floor. Tish had a great brute of a typewriter and reams of paper in her flat; Flossie had tinware, paints, and an even greater brute of an oven in hers. Both were at work on their trades, but were delighted to take a break and welcome me. Both gave me a more feminine version of Harold's inquisitive look, and both in unison asked the question he would not. "Enola, what on earth are you up to?"

With a sweeping gesture and a heroic lift of my chin I told them, "I seek the brethren of the street."

"Excuse me?" said Flossie.

"Whatever do you mean?" asked Tish.

I admitted, "I have no idea," then turned to Flossie. "I need to be inconspicuous for a long period of time in the neighbourhood behind the Strand, so I've come to ask a favour: might I borrow a street peddler's gear, and some orphaned japanware?"

Both burst out laughing, then hastened to help me.

Tish found the tray I needed to sling from my shoulders, and Flossie provided me with two bags full of brightly painted tinware trinkets to display upon it: tiny treasure chests, button boxes, match holders, whatnot trays, posy vases, and the like. Because she was a free spirit and painted what she liked on her wares, Flossie always had on hand a number of "orphans," items that simply would not sell because she had decorated them with frogs or cacti or harpies or erupting volcanoes as opposed to the customary roses and cherubs. I sometimes purchased her more alarming creations to give to Sherlock.

Complete with supplies, then, I took thankful leave of the Glover twins and had Harold drive me to the area I was interested in, and let me out on a deserted cul-de-sac so that I might not be seen; street peddlers did not generally travel in cabs. At the last minute, because they were not terribly comfortable, I placed inside my cheeks and nostrils the rubber inserts that rounded out my features and helped me look not quite so much like a horse-faced aristocrat.

"Shall I come looking for you in an hour, Miss Enola?" asked Harold, placing my bags on the pavement.

"Not at all, Harold. I expect I shall be all day."

Nevertheless, an hour later I saw him drive by. As I stood displaying a tray full of dubious tinware on a corner of a narrow road called Smutty Lane, quite near to where the mad dog was said to have attacked Wolcott Balestier, I saw Harold checking on me, and ignored him.

I suppose he wanted to keep me out of the hands of riffraff. As I had often observed in London, a street a block away from another might be entirely different in character, and indeed, this narrow thoroughfare behind the Savoy was quite different from the avenue running parallel to it, the Strand. Here, the kerbs were broken in places, and dirt was as plentiful as either cobbles or paving-stones. Children quite unattached to any visible adult swarmed hither and yon. An ill-assorted kind of man swaggered past me with a parrot on his shoulder, the bird parting his long hair with its beak to nibble his ear. A shabby woman with only one eyebrow extending across her entire forehead stopped to inspect my wares. A man wearing sandwich boards advertising hair lotion shuffled past. "Tinware! Fine tinware, cheap!" I called, as I had to remember to do from time to time, and he gave me a friendly glance. I noticed his idle hands hanging down, and thought how naked they seemed without gloves. I also noticed that the back of one hand was slightly injured.

His bare hands advertised him as a commoner, for one hardly ever saw a gentleman in a public place without gloves. Even a gentleman who has fallen upon hard times will still wear gloves, very likely patched at the finger ends, and will sit without crossing his legs so as not to reveal the holes in the soles of his shoes. I had seldom enough seen my brother Sherlock's long and faultlessly aristocratic hands revealed without gloves. Hazily thinking along these lines—for when one is on the lookout for one knows not what, one must trust such notions—I began watching people's hands and feet. I saw a fleshy man with square, cushiony hands almost like paws, and for some reason I wondered whether he was a baker. Sherlock would know. But even without Sherlock I could tell a stone quarrier by his hobnailed boots and his hands so large and strong I could not imagine them ever fitting into an aristocrat's slender gloves. A woman pushing assorted small children in a perambulator went past, her hands quite lacking gloves of any kind at all, and I saw with a slight shudder that her fingernails were black-rimmed with grime. How had she gotten her hands almost as grubby as those of a little girl who was presently tracing with her finger in the dirt near my feet? The child drew what looked like a house, but then put a head and feet on it.

"What's that?" I asked.

She turned to grin up at me. "I don't know!" she sang.

Playing along, I coaxed, "No, please, do tell!"

"Can't. It's a secret."

"You can tell *me*." I gave a coy look.

Her eyes grew very round, and she stood up to face me, saying in a hoarse whisper, "Thick new man!"

A boy running past stopped abruptly to tell her, "Hush your mouth!" and to rub out the drawing with his exceedingly scuffed boot. The girl, indignant, cried out and smacked him ineffectually, then ran. He chased her. I wondered what he thought was so wrong with her crude picture of a thick man, new or otherwise. Thick new man?

I shrugged. "Tinware! Fine tinware, cheap!" I called in a carefully Cockney voice.

A few women stopped to look at my wares, and one

of them actually purchased a match holder with flames painted on it. Then a common labourer inspected them, picking up and putting down each item in turn. "Need to get something for my wife," he muttered. His fingernails were ragged as well as being dirty, and one of his rough, muscular hands had a kind of scab or perhaps a burn running up its back.

"What happened to your hand?" I asked.

"Nothing." Quite abruptly he went away.

His injury had seemed similar to that of the man wearing the sandwich boards. Might it have something to do with their both having performed the same job in some factory, perhaps?

The day began to seem long, many and various people passed, and I lunched on gingerbread I had brought along with me in my pocket, and then of course I grew thirsty. I was tempted by a colourful "cooling drink" from a vendor with a barrel on a donkey cart, but decided against it, both from mistrust of the beverage and foresight regarding my personal functions; where would I find a privy?

Time grew more tedious by the minute. A few more pedestrians stopped to look at Flossie's wares, and a large, old woman with seemingly no lips (due to the compressed way she folded her mouth) purchased a pair of bright red candlesticks. (Flossie preferred Chinese red to the more customary black enamel.) I yawned, fidgeted, and kept on taking hazy note of the people who frequented this street. Mostly working class, I decided, and many of them struggling, judging by the state of their clothes and their teeth. But I saw only a very few beggars, and only a very few kid-gloved gentry either; most of the folk hereabouts earned their bread with their bare, strong, rough, and great-knuckled hands. . . .

"Lemme 'ave your 'and, sissy!" shrilled a treble voice nearby.

Blinking, I looked down on two small ragamuffin boys, only one of them with a battered excuse for a hat on his head, squatting in the dirt near my feet.

"This way!" The one with the hat grabbed the other boy's hand in both of his. Fiercely and rapidly he scratched his thumbnail up and down the back of the other boy's fist.

"Stop it! Yer taking the skin off!" protested the other.

"Of course, stupid, it's got to leave a mark."

"I don't like it! It hurts!"

Indeed, I could see, the strange proceedings were about to draw blood. The afflicted boy struggled to pull free of the other one, who bellowed at him, "If you wanna be thick new man I gotta do this!"

"Who said I wanted to!" The boy jerked free and ran away, the other one ran after him, and I stood staring after them with my mouth open.

Then I shut my mouth and shifted my gaze to the people in the street, picking out the artisans and labourers, scanning their hands. The foot traffic roiled so much that I saw something only for an instant and at a distance, on the other side of the street, but there it was: a vertical red mark on the skin on the back of some common fellow's hand.

Pressing my lips together, I nodded, then gratefully packed the tinware into my bags and folded my tray to depart. The afternoon was only half gone, but I considered that I was finished with this place for the time being. Quite publicly and shamelessly I removed the rubber inserts from my cheeks and nostrils as I left; I would not return in this guise again. Perhaps, just possibly, I thought and hoped, I had found a clue regarding "the brethren of the street."

• • •

Flossie, laughingly glad of the small sum of money I turned over to her, then invited me to join her and Tish for an early dinner of pie and mash and jellied eels—the most inexpensive of dishes, and surely the most undignified. With each mouthful of eel, one must first suck the flesh of the fish off of the spine, then spit out the bone. I gladly accepted, the three of us had great fun over our shared meal, and on my way home, I stopped at the telegraph office to send this wire to my brother Sherlock:

HAVE YOU FOUND MARY ERASMUS STOP URGENT
I SPEAK WITH HER STOP ENOLA

• • •

Then I returned to the Professional Women's Club, because I had to change clothes before I went to visit Caroline Balestier.

I had decided to do this for tangled reasons. I was tired of knowing she thought poorly of me. It has never been my custom to let bad enough alone. And I rather liked her, actually, for her sarcastic tendencies and the way she lifted her chin. Also, I thought of what she was going through and felt for her. And, being merely a blighted female upon the earth as she was, I felt myself to be, in a sense, her sister.

I faced my wardrobe and deplored my recent slaughter of my two best dresses. Given my fashion taste, or lack of any, it was difficult for me to dress up without appearing flamboyant. However, by putting together an uncharacteristically simple blouse with a plain, narrow skirt, I managed it. My boater having been trampled, I borrowed a similar straw hat from the advice columnist next door, and, donning grey kidskin gloves and carrying a meek drawstring reticule, off I went.

The sun was just setting. Even if Caroline Balestier had once again gone to some public place in order to display her brother's picture and appeal to passers-by, surely she would return home once it became too dark for anyone to see the likeness properly.

By taking a cab, then the Underground, then another cab, I arrived at the Balestiers' Maiden Lane address shortly after nightfall. I could see lamplight through the windows. Someone was home.

At the front door, feeling some slight trepidation, I knocked.

I heard a ponderous tread approaching. The parlour-maid opened the door, then started as if a crocodile stood before her. Pop-eyed, she gasped at me, "How dare you!"

She had heard about me, evidently. My trepidation was justified.

However, I trust my face showed no response. Coolly and sweetly I asked, "Is Lady Balestier in?"

My promotion of Miss Balestier to Lady, I think, prevented the parlour-maid from slamming the door in my face. She stood speechless, boggling at me.

Feeling that her disposition was unlikely to improve any further, I strode forward and breezed, or rather squeezed (for the parlour-maid was a portly barrier) into the house, heading towards the firelight I saw coming from the back parlour. The well-to-do will light a hearth fire after nightfall even in the summertime, for the sake of its comforting associations.

Caroline Balestier, black-clad, nestled like a shadow

deep in the largest armchair, apparently oblivious to the scene that had just taken place on her doorstep, her dark eyes blank and open, unseeing. She did not notice me until I spoke.

"Miss Balestier, I have come to bring you some news of your brother, if I may."

She came to life like a startled wildcat, bolting upright with a fierce stare fixed on me, but then, seeming to take in what I had just said, she demanded, "What do you mean?"

The parlour-maid cannoned in to protect her mistress, but Carrie Balestier dismissed her with an upraised hand, not even looking at her, only at me. "What do you mean, news of my brother?" she insisted.

"Just that." Without waiting for an invitation to be seated, I settled onto an ottoman near her feet in order to make myself no longer taller than her; I looked upward to face her. "I have learned, at least in part, what might have happened to him."

Her eyes yearned, but her chin jutted out. "And what do you hope to gain by approaching me in this impertinent way?"

"Nothing! I expect nothing in return. It is just

that . . ." I softened my tone. "I am female, like you, and I imagine that the men have told you very little, if anything at all."

Her lips parted, causing her chin to retract. She said wryly, "No, they quite wish to spare me," and our eyes met with a certain measure of understanding.

I nodded. "It is dreadful to be 'spared.'"

She gave a small nod. "Quite. I would far prefer to suffer in knowledge rather than in ignorance." Her voice was most distinctive, rather low for a woman, and with her American accent softening all of her consonants, rather pleasant, like a viola among violins. "Tell me, what has happened to my brother?"

I took a deep breath. "The theory regarding book pirates has been debunked. The facts are these: Thursday night, as your brother walked near the Savoy on the Strand, he courageously attempted to club a mad dog with his cane, but did not succeed. The dog bit him in his lower leg."

She gasped, and her hands flew to comfort her face. A log in the fire fell with a crash and a shower of sparks. The silence afterwards felt like a scream.

I rushed to speak. "I have two witnesses. A woman

selling boutonnieres, and one serving in General Booth's spiritual army."

"But—but . . ." Caroline Balestier could barely speak. "He was hurt? But how badly? Why didn't he come home? A *dog bite*?" Her eyes widened as her mind struggled to comprehend, peeling away layers as if tragedy were an onion. "A mad dog? A *rabid* dog?" Tears gathered in her eyes, and she choked on the words.

"He need not die of rabies," I told her with the greatest of staunch British fortitude. "There is, at least in France, a new and very hopeful treatment. It is called an inoculation."

She scarcely seemed to hear me. "But why did he not come *home*?" she protested, fighting not to weep.

No longer able to meet her eyes, I looked down and spoke to the oriental carpet. "It would seem that some people are preventing him from doing so."

"People? What people?"

"That I do not yet know. But I must find out." Because I could not be of any better help to her, something more than the hearth fire heated my face, and I scrambled up from my low seat to flee.

"The instant I learn something of them, I will tell you." I all but ran towards the door.

"Wait!" she called, springing to her feet. "What is your name?"

"I must spare you that knowledge," I said, keeping my voice too low for her to hear, for she did not wish to be spared. The next moment, I was past the front door and whisking down the pavement, lost from sight in the darkness.

Chapter the Tenth

Early the next day, Wednesday, the maid brought in, along with matutinal hot water, a replying telegram from Sherlock:

NO JOY STOP NO POLICE REPORTS OF CANINE
INSANITY STOP MOST PERPLEXING

"No joy"? I wondered if Sherlock had ever, even once in his life actually ridden with a fox hunt. I also considered that it was high time for "tally ho." It had been almost a week since Wolcott Balestier disappeared. I must, simply must, track down Mary Erasmus today, because she knew something! Why else would she have given me a false name? Ethel Etheridge, my eye.

Skipping breakfast (not something I would normally do!), I clothed myself simply, with a scarf tied over my head in lieu of a hat, and set forth quite early. I reached the Covent Garden Flower Market at the height of morning bustle, went directly to the vendors of day-old flowers at the bottom of the market, and started asking, "Excuse me, have you seen Mary Erasmus?"

The fifth vendor I asked, a harried and rather hairy woman of uncertain age, answered without even looking up to see what I was about, "She should be here any minute."

And so she was.

I watched Mary Erasmus, stoutly corseted and looking upholstered as before, approach through the crowd with a big, empty basket on her arm and what looked like a genuine smile on her flat face. Rather than confronting her, I thought, I would learn more from her if I could keep her smiling, so when I stepped forwards to intercept her, I greeted her lightly, almost in jest. "Ethel Etheridge, you are a sobriquet!"

Startled only slightly, she acknowledged, "An incognito."

"An alias!"

Playfully sparring with vocabulary, we stood like two rocks in the middle of a flowery flow, people from all directions parting to pass us.

"A pseudonym."

"An anonym."

"A nom de guerre."

"A name of war? I admit defeat," said I with a smile. "Pray tell, how did you come to acquire your victorious vocabulary?" Anything I might learn of her could do me only good.

She replied amiably enough, "My mother was a ragged schoolteacher."

Ragged school! From such struggling beginnings came the scholars of the streets, and sometimes the leaders, or the rebels.

"And she was the proud owner of a dictionary," added "Ethel Etheridge."

I cocked my head. "Was there a bit of a competition with your mother?" I inquired, remembering my own illustrious mum.

"A bit," she conceded.

Yes. I knew I had recognised something in her.

"Are your parents still alive?"

"No." Her amiability vanished.

But I persisted. "So, you are on your own? Can you support yourself by selling boutonnieres?"

"Hardly. By day, I am an artisan in fingernail lacquer." Interesting! A recent fad, nail lacquer was much in demand among the wealthy, although why any woman should want to glorify her fingernails only to hide them in multi-button gloves was beyond my understanding. "I concoct, sell, and apply my own product," continued Mary Erasmus with a proud lift of the head. "I am as much of an entrepreneur as any factory owner."

I heard heavy scorn in those last words. She considered herself to be quite above common labour and far more than what society saw her for, evidently. I studied her, feeling one of my mad mental connexions forming within my mind.

"So, Miss Nom de Guerre," I asked with a teasing smile, "what is the name of your war?"

With fire in her words she said, "The war to keep

the streets near the Embankment safe for the folk who live there."

"Ah." I nodded, hesitating—but yes, I realised, utterly without my brother's kind of logic, my mind had divined, and I must take the risk. I said, "Hence, thick new man?"

"Yes, oh yes!" Where had her scorn gone? Her sudden enthusiasm surprised me so much that my smile almost slipped. She crowed, "I, myself, thought of that as the most apt of all possible names, you know! They're sacred guardians in Egypt and other hot parts of the world. They eat crocodile eggs. They kill poisonous snakes. They are the perfect symbol for defense of the safety of the village."

I blinked, because, even though she was clearly speaking the Queen's English, I couldn't seem to understand a word she was saying. "I'm sorry, what is so perfect?"

"Thick new mans!"

I continued to stand there blank and blinking, utterly at a loss—so much so that Mary Erasmus a.k.a. Ethel Etheridge actually stamped one of her fat but daintily booted feet. "The mark!" she exploded at me.

"The recruits, what they do to their hands, it's called the mark of thick new man, which to me sounds infinitely better than mongoose!"

I almost asked if a thick new man must possess a goose before, finally, understanding struck me: mongoose. She was referring to a kind of Egyptian mongoose, for the love of folly. Comprehension banged me so hard, as if my lagging faculties were a great gong, that I clasped my head between my hands. "The mark of the ichneumon," I bleated.

"Yes! Yes, the brotherhood swears by the Mark of the Ichneumon to guard their beleaguered neighbourhood."

The men with marks on their hands were, indeed, the brethren of the streets.

"And they are your friends," I ventured. "Indeed, they are your followers." This interesting woman had a large streak of outlaw leader in her; I felt sure of it.

But no matter how mild my tone, I had gone too far. My quarry startled like a spooked horse, eyes wide and white, stepping back from me.

I spread my hands palms down and bespoke her soothingly. "Now, don't go off half-cocked. I have no desire to detain you from purchasing your flowers, Mary."

Alas, she leapt as if I were a cobra, then stood poised like the veriest mongoose ready to attack, as I realised my error: I had spoken her real name.

So I spoke it again. "Mary," I begged before she could go off completely cocked, "I only want to know what happened to my friend who was bitten by the mad dog."

"Now, they 'ad to put 'im away for safety, dint they?" she cried, suddenly stridently Cockney, and snake-quick she hurled her big basket at me, with expertise I could hardly have expected: the handle passed neatly over the top of my head and settled behind my neck so that the basket itself remained propped in front of my face like a mask. I could see only woven mesh, and disturbingly, I heard a hubbub of raised and querulous voices all around me, drawing away from me rather than coming forwards to help me. Suddenly quite alone in my very own clearing of the crowded flower market, I managed with some difficulty to lift the basket off of my head and look around me. Mary Erasmus was, of course, nowhere in sight.

I suppose I should have been grateful to possess a lovely new basket. However, I took it to the harried woman vendor and handed it over. "You will return it to Mary?"

It would seem so, for she accepted the basket, yet she neither looked at me nor spoke. With a sigh, I left, walking out of Covent Garden Flower Market and away, along the pavements of the milling, soot-filled city.

"They," the mysterious brotherhood, "had to put him away for safety." What on earth did that mean? Where was Wolcott Balestier?

Evidently, I could not, or at least not at this time, find him with any help from Mary Erasmus. Therefore, what to do? The day was still young.

In somewhat less than a ladylike mood, I shrilly whistled for the first cab I saw, and gave the startled driver a Baker Street address.

But when I got there, my famous brother was not at home, and I felt too uncertain in my mind to leave him any note. Botheration.

Back at my club but wishing I had somewhere worthier to go, I changed my shabby clothes for a cleaner and more fashionable frock. Because the best way to think is sometimes to distract oneself from thinking, I joined some others in the morning room and partook of polite conversation, weak coffee, a cold lamb sandwich and a cucumber one, then no less than three sponge cakes. Then, still not exactly thinking about Wolcott Balestier but subliminally searching for some way to find him, I strolled through the library (more research?), the tea room (read tea leaves?), card room (did he gamble? Doubtful), sitting room (I had been in his; had it helped at all?), and the parlour, empty at this time of day, where I stood eye to eye with myself reflected in a gilt-framed mirror. Regarding my own pale and bony face steadily, I spoke aloud:

"See here, Enola, what angle have you not yet pursued? You have traced Cotswold's movements as far as the dog attack. You have questioned two female witnesses and found them less than helpful. The so-called Mark of the ridiculous Ichneumon seems to have taken Cotswold, but I am sure they are sworn to secrecy. The police? Sherlock has talked with them. . . ."

At that point I ceased speaking, for I felt a curious sense that my brain was gathering itself, for all the world like a frog residing inside my head, to make one of its peculiarly rash, illogical, and illuminating leaps. Words floated to mind:

NO POLICE REPORTS OF CANINE INSANITY

MOST PERPLEXING

And I grinned, made a horrid face at myself in the mirror, then whirled away to get to work.

One of the parties most deeply involved in Balestier's disappearance had been neglected, with only feeble attempts to trace it having been made. It remained to be tracked down, and its whereabouts might possibly have some bearing on the case.

That party was the mad dog itself.

. . .

Two rather rigourous hours later, I had made my way back to the same corner of Smutty Lane as the day before, this time not as a tinware vendor, but as a genteel and eccentric lady artist wearing an enormous feather-trimmed purple hat. My good Harold carried for me a three-legged folding stool to which I had managed to attach a carriage parasol. On this stool and under this shelter from the sun I sat, occupying more than my share of the pavement whilst exhibiting the characteristic indifference that displayed how upper-class I was. Having taken position and instructed Harold to come back later, I opened the selfsame portable drawing kit my mother had given me years ago, on my fourteenth birthday. Then, taking pencil in lilac-gloved hand, I proceeded to sketch my view of the street, acting blandly oblivious to curious passers-by who lagged, then loitered, then became onlookers.

Quickly outlining the buildings, the lamp poles, the shop signs, and the corner pillar-box where one could post letters, I neglected to include people. Instead, I drew quite a spirited rendition of the rabid dog.

A man standing over me exclaimed in heightened tones, "That's the mad dog wot's been giving a fright to the Hembankment!"

Ignoring him, I pushed the sketch aside and started another, this one devoted to the rabid dog, and nothing else, with great specificity. The black Alsatian was quite distinguishable from, say, a chow, a greyhound, or a curly-haired spaniel.

Stifled cries and murmurs arose all around my shoulders, and the same man told the top of my head more loudly, "That's the mad dog wot bit a man last week!"

Whilst maintaining apparent indifference, inwardly I chortled with glee, and couldn't wait to tell Harold how beautifully my plein-air-artist ploy had worked, whereas, if I had simply walked into that neighbourhood, shown a poster, and pressed inquiries, not a single soul would have told me a thing.

After a moment, I condescended to glance up at the excitable man and respond, "Is that so?"

From my seated angle I looked straight up the large nostrils of his nose, which were quite hirsute and so interesting that I had to exhort myself to pay attention to what he was saying.

"Yes, it's so!" he declared. "Three days the brute ran wild before they managed to take care of it."

My mind gibbered like monkeys in a bucket, but I kept my voice almost bored. "They?"

Up spoke someone else, a woman. "Me cousin and his friend done it! Brave men they be!"

I inquired, "They killed it?"

"No! No, the copper bobbies could've been called to do that." She sounded scornful.

"Why call the coppers when there's twenty pounds to be had for taking it alive?" put in yet another voice, this time the slightly arrogant one of a young man. "Me and me cousin," he bragged, "we undertook to catch it in a great net and take it to the chap in Shoreditch. Twenty pounds he gave us, and we earned it, every penny, for dangerous work it was. The brute beast raged—"

I put in, "Chap in Shoreditch?"

"Why, the chap who pays for the mad dogs and such, you know."

I knew nothing of the sort, and for the first time allowed myself a note of interest. "He *does*?"

A veritable chorus of voices, both male and female, responded.

". . . big old estate wot fills a whole block in Shoreditch."

"Sure and lord only knows why anyone would want a mad dog, but we ask no questions, the money being what it is."

"Nobody kills the mad dogs anymore; we takes them there, because he pays handsome for them."

". . . Shellacker's Place off Roxton . . ."

"Dr. Lister's place in Shoreditch."

Dr. Lister? Hadn't Florence Nightingale mentioned a Lord Joseph Lister who took a political interest in rabies?

• • •

Now there seemed scarcely enough time left in the day. Entrusting my art paraphernalia to Harold, I had him drop me at the Underground, for my destination would have taken hours for him and his loyal nag, Brownie, to reach. I would far rather have ventured to this teeming, disreputable area just outside of London with Harold, of course, but must needs.

Thus, alas, it was from the front of a stranger's hansom that I first saw Shoreditch, and there I perceived the same sad story I knew from the East End of London: homes had been torn down and factories built, folk had poured in to work at the latter, few rooms were to be had and rents were high, folk lived a dozen to a chamber or else on the street, and the town had fallen into decrepitude. My cab jounced over broken cobbles between dilapidated Georgian buildings, the street crowded by teeming people and the open-air stalls of costermongers. I found myself to be fair game in a hansom when an unruly mob of beggars implored me from all sides. I was unwise enough to throw pennies to them, whilst at the same time my cabbie urged his horse into a trot to leave them behind. We proceeded a few blocks farther, and then, in a far less populous area, we halted.

"This be it," the driver said.

"This, what?" I asked, for I faced nothing except a singularly tall, plain, pallid, and unlovely wall built not of brick but, rather, of large blocks of Portland cement, I believe they call it.

"I can't find no Shellacker's Place 'cept this."

"Where is the entrance?" I felt like adding, "You dullard!" But I didn't, and he obliged me by driving on, looking for a door of some sort. The wall, eight feet tall and topped by wrought-iron spikes, enclosed an entire city block, with nothing to be seen behind it except treetops. However, if this was where people brought mad dogs, I could understand why it must needs be such a fortress.

Then, from my cab I saw a couple of men standing on the pavement outside the Portland cement wall, not gentlemen but quite common fellows, one of them carrying a burlap sack that squirmed and wiggled. Noticing that he held this item out to one side and far from his legs, I blinked a few times, signaled my cabbie to stop, paid my fare plus a goodly tip through the slot in the ceiling, then stepped out and watched the cab roll away.

When I turned, the fellows with the burlap sack were watching *me*. The shorter, stocky one wore a suit of a rather alarming checkerboard weave; the taller one, who bore the bag, had trousers held up by a length of rope. Evidently they were of the humblest labouring class. "Hello," I remarked as if I were meeting them there for a reason. "Lovely day, is it not?"

They did not answer, but neither did they run away or attack me.

I nodded at the sack and asked in the friendliest of tones, "What do you have there?"

"Good an' proper nun," one replied with a good and proper Cockney accent.

Now, of all ciphers and secret codes, the one I can least understand is Cockney rhyming slang. I knew that

"'Ave a butcher's" meant "have a look," because "look" rhymed with "hook" and butchers used hooks to hang meat on. I knew that "hive of bees" referred to money because bees make honey and "honey" rhymed with "money." "Great plates" meant big feet ("plates of meat" rhymed with "feet"), but beyond that I found myself boggled. Good and proper nun?

But there are times when one mustn't mind being an ignoramus. Arching my eyebrows to their utmost, I fluted in my best mock-aristocratic manner, "I beg your pardon, but what sort of nun, exactly, might you have in your bag?"

They grinned, and the second one condescended to clarify. "Rabbit."

Oh. Nuns had habits which rhymed with "rabbits." *Of course,* I thought sarcastically.

"Rabbit rabbit," rejoined the first one, or at least I thought that was what he said. But then, as he grimaced and thrust the bag even farther away from himself, I felt a frisson of horror. "Oh," I murmured.

Rabid rabbit. They were delivering a rabbit infected with rabies to the place where rabid animals were taken for some purpose I did not yet understand. And this place housed quite a fortified undertaking, judging by the wall looming over us.

Just as I thought this, a grinding noise close at hand startled me, and part of the wall—or what I had thought was part of the wall—swung outwards. What looked like a large block of Portland cement opened, revealing itself as a secret door pushed outwards by a man—no, a person—no, a rather formidable woman who shouted at the men with the bag, "What is it, now?"

(She shouted for good reason. Her voice was almost drowned out by the noise of many barking, yelping, yapping dogs issuing from behind her.)

"Nun," answered the taller one succinctly.

"Mad?"

"Quite."

"Oh, good. We can always use more mad nuns." Hearing humour in her voice, I liked her despite the shocking fact that her hair was hacked short, and moreover she wore no hat! Her apparel could not have been more rudimentary: brown cotton dress, tan apron, and on her feet, big, rubbery galoshes. With large hands gloved in coarse canvas she handed coinage to the men, and then, with all due care, took the sack from them.

They left. I remained. Holding the burlap bag at arm's length, the short-haired woman (and how very odd it was that she should flout convention so!) turned her plain, blunt face towards me and stared.

"Is Dr. Lister in?" I asked.

"Not yet. Later." She stepped back and started to shut me out.

I stepped forwards to prevent her doing so, thus putting myself perilously close to the writhing sack of rabid rabbit. "May I come in and wait?"

"There's no place to wait."

From out of one of my lilac-coloured gloves I produced money in paper, Bank of England form. "May I come in anyway?"

Her stare intensified.

Almost diffidently I found myself explaining, "One likes to learn things about, um, things."

"Not faint-hearted, are ye?"

"No."

"One of them Suffragists, might ye be?"

"Yes."

"All right, then. Keep yer money," she added ungraciously, turning her back and striding off with her nun-in-a-sack. "Shut the door," she added over her shoulder.

I did so and followed her into stinking pande-monium.

• • •

Tapping out that word "pandemonium" on my very modern typewriting machine, I realise that it means, actually, "demons everywhere," and such was the sensation I experienced whilst venturing amidst dozens of snarling, barking, leaping dogs—all kinds; hounds, mastiffs, set-ters, pointers, and sheerest mongrels—separated from me only by wrought-iron kennel railings. Please under-stand that I love dogs, as witness my darling old Regi-nald Collie—but it would seem that when one multiplies anything, even something as harmless as ducklings, to the magnitude of a mob, it becomes fearsome. Espe-cially as, in the midst of the enclosure of large dogs, was the very most fearsome—a huge, wire-haired bear of a dog—frenzied, foaming at the mouth, and lunging to attack the others.

I stopped short. "Mad dog!" I cried, pointing.

Pausing with her galoshes planted in the midst of

overflowing muck near a water pump, the woman-of-all-work gave me a look clearly telling me I should have expected that very thing. But she said only, "They brought him in yesterday."

"They?" I demanded. "The Mark of the Ichneumon?"

Her heavy brows rose. "Aye. How d'you know?"

"Never mind. Why did they bring you the dog? Aren't you going to do away with it?"

"Kill it, you mean?" With a challenging look she used that very stark and bold word. "Kill it? No need. Only may it live long enough to thoroughly bite the others."

My mouth hung open but failed to form any sensible questions.

She raised her eyes heavenward in a display of lost patience, jerked her head at me, said, "Come on," and trudged off between the many shade trees. Turning my back with a shudder on the enclosure full of doomed dogs, I followed her with wrinkled nose—the stench of the place was overwhelming—past what seemed to be kenneling. I saw a water trough at one end of a half-walled structure, straw-filled beds like shelves along the sides, and flagstone floors sloping down to a full, utterly filthy and stinking gutter in the middle. We then passed a similar kennel filled with smaller dogs of all shapes and sizes yapping at us through the barred doors and windows. Then came sheds full of empty cages, and crazily shuttered outbuildings made, like the walls, of Portland cement, buildings of which I could not guess the purpose—and finally we came to a monstrous big rabbit hutch.

"Nuns," I said when I saw windows full of long-eared bunnies.

As she walked ahead of me, I could see only my guide's back, but I heard her give a snort that might have been a laugh.

Emboldened, I asked, "What is your name, if you please?"

"And if I don't please?" But, unlatching a gate, she turned and gave me a not unfriendly look. "It's Maud, if you must know. And yours?"

I told her. She nodded. "Enoler," she repeated, then thrust the burlap bag of rabid rabbit at me. "Hold this, would you?"

Not faint-hearted, I reminded myself, accepting it. Stiffly I suspended the wriggling sack as far from myself as I could, watching as Maud walked through the gate into an enclosure that once might have been grassy. Crouching beside the hutch, she unlatched several small, low doors, and rabbits emerged in their uniquely cautious and jumpy way—peeking out, hesitant, with soft noses all aquiver, then venturing to leap forth—rabbits almost as various as the dogs, white or brown or particoloured, fuzzy or smooth, some with lop ears hanging down. Maud waited patiently until they all came out. She treated the animals much the same way she treated me; she seemed not unfriendly. Walking through rabbits, she shuffled so as not to kick them. After closing the hutch doors again, she let herself out of the gate, positioning her large and unlovely feet so as to prevent the bunnies from escaping. Then, with a grimace, she took the sack away from me and turned to hold it over the enclosure. "Now, then," she said in warning tones as, deftly and quite swiftly, with her heavily gloved hands she grasped the sack by the bottom instead of the top, upending it.

The darkly foam-slicked, thrashing thing that leapt out, all teeth and eyes, so little resembled any ordinary rabbit that I jumped back and I believe I screamed, but one could not hear; all the rabbits were shrieking.

"Don't look," Maud stolidly advised. "Come along. I must do my work."

Once again, shuddering, I followed her. She trudged back to the empty kennel, took a rectangular sort of scraper shovel that was leaning against the wall, and began to address the abominably stinky solid waste that dogs produce. I picked up another such shovel and joined her.

"I don't need help," she complained.

"I never said you did."

"Them fancy gloves ain't going to protect yer hands much."

"Bother my hands. I want to ask you, has there been a black Alsatian here lately?"

She gave me a look that was blank to the soul. While not exactly simple, I would venture to say, Maud seemed to be no scholar.

"A big black dog with pointy ears."

"Yerself has pointy ears," she complained. And, as I worked with my shovel, "If you must mess with the poo, don't break it up. Try to keep it whole. It's easier to gather that way."

"*Gather* it?" I had rather thought we were getting rid of the stinky stuff!

"The tanner will be here with tubs for it shortly."

"The *tanner*?"

"To use it fer pure to make leather with! Enoler, don't you know nuthin'?"

"No. I don't. I don't understand anything. For heaven's sake, why are you letting the rabid animals bite the others?"

She gave me a look that stated as plainly as words that I was a born idiot. "To give them rabies."

"But *why*?"

She gave me the same look, only louder. "So when they die, we can dry their brains."

Chapter the Eleventh

We then worked in silence for some moments. My own brain, neither rabid nor dried but brought to a standstill when faced with Maud, could formulate no more questions.

I was considering how best to retire with dignity from the field of dog poo when a great uproar of barking broke out from the other kennel, giving me reason to cease work, turn around, and see a gentleman in a well-made but rather ill-fitting frock-coat and trousers walking towards us between the trees. The lowering light, turning murky amber as the day neared sundown, gilded him like a monument. As he neared, I could see that he was quite an impressively leonine elderly man, stooped but strong, his considerable jaw sticking out amidst an unruly mane of white hair. It scarcely detracted that he, like many other males, chose to shave his chin and lips but let wings of fluff sprout from the sides of his face. Such topiary of the whiskers always looked absurd to me, every bit as silly as the feathery feminine hats such men were wont to laugh at, but this particular gentleman possessed a humble dignity that made up for any eccentricity.

"Maud, what is all this?" he asked mildly. A tilt of his head seemed to indicate that "all this" meant me.

Pausing in her work—as had I—Maud faced him with a hint of a smile. "You mean the young lydy, Doctor? I can't rightly say. She just come a-visiting, like a cat might, you know."

I alerted like a bird dog. "Dr. Lister?" I blurted.

"Yes?" He turned his eyes on me, remarkably pale blue-grey eyes set deep beneath exceedingly shaggy eyebrows that were pure white. His face, hair, eyes, all loomed oddly pale above his dark waistcoat and thin black bow tie.

I told him, "I am trying to track down a black Alsatian that perhaps was brought here?"

He had white eyelashes, too, I noticed as he looked on me in surprise. "A rabid dog?"

"Yes."

"You wish to find the dog?"

"In order to find a missing gentleman. After he was bitten by the dog, he most unaccountably disappeared."

He nodded, still looking puzzled, but kind even though the corners of his mouth insisted on turning down. "Come with me. What is your name?"

I told him as I walked beside him to one of the buildings made of Portland cement, and he opened the door—an odd door, very plain but made of metal, not wood. Dr. Lister guided me in and lit the largest gas lamp I had ever seen, five globes mounted on a sort of wheel suspended from the ceiling above a table. Throughout the large room, other such gas lamps illuminated other such tables—but they were not really tables, not in any dining room sense of the word. Rather, they were narrow metal structures—I should call them slabs—around which a few young men in white coats were working.

But upon the smooth slab to which Dr. Lister had led me, beneath the bright gas lamp, lay—the black Alsatian! I felt myself blanch, but then saw that its eyes, wide open, had no life in them. It was dead.

Inert and motionless, it looked so unlike the ravening monster I had seen that I leaned over it for a closer look.

"Do not touch it," warned Dr. Lister. "It may be deadly even now. My theory is that the *saliva*, not merely the bite as such, conveys the vital agency, or germ, or whatever one cares to call it. . . ." He hesitated as if afraid he might be boring me.

"This may be the dog of which I spoke," I told him, keeping most of my excited feelings out of my tone. "How came it here?"

"Why, it was brought in on—let me see—three days ago, and lapsed into a coma, dying earlier today. As soon as I can, now, I must open its head to remove its brain and spinal cord."

My own poor brain, not quite comatose but thoroughly flummoxed, echoed what Maud had said: "So when they die we can dry their brains."

"Why?" I blurted. "What for?"

His whole face brightened, and he spoke quite eagerly. "Because I am convinced rabies travels through the nervous system to settle in the brain—although it's not really the brain I use so much in my experiments as the spinal cord, but the most effective way to extract it is by pulling it out with the brain. Then, after being removed from the animal, it must be most scrupulously dried. Here, let me show you." Taking me by the arm, he led me out of that building and through the vaguely golden murk that substituted, in the city, for sunset—definitely, it was getting late and I was missing dinner—Dr. Lister escorted me towards another of his very modern buildings. I looked around me and asked no questions, for Dr. Lister had a great deal to tell me, chatting to me the whole time about miasmas and stench and how it was insufficient to think that they, in and of themselves, spread disease, how necessary it was to fix upon some more specific agent of infestation. And how he had all but proven this exact point by practicing scrupulous cleanliness and the use of carbolic acid to keep wounds from becoming septic when he practiced surgery. And—

And he interrupted himself to say, "Here we are." He opened the plain metal door to one of those buildings I had noticed before, all crazily shuttered, its walls entirely given over to slatted windows I did not understand until Dr. Lister added, "This is one of the drying houses, with louvres for ventilation."

Oh. Oh, my stars and garters. My mouth frankly agape, I stared above and around me at what looked like thousands of Japanese lanterns made of plain brown parcel paper, translucent shapes like box kites hanging. Suspended in the middle of each one I saw an odd, wrinkled kind of creature with a long, dangling tail.

But it wasn't creatures and their tails. It was brains and spinal cords. Hundreds of them, large and small, dog and rabbit and truly I had no idea what else. All neatly labeled with dates and other information, some of them fat and some more and more shriveled, all in various stages of desiccation.

"Each container includes potassium," said Lister, "to make sure of truly dry air, and—what one is trying to do is quite complicated, really, one must refine the virulence through one rabbit after another, and it is frightfully experimental, hundreds of tests to be run. But when all is done, in the rather uncertain end, one hopes that one can harvest bits of the dried spinal cord and then, in the

cleanliest of all possible conditions, grind them into pow-
der which, when suspended in water made sterile by boiling, might most providentially provide an inoculation."

That word, still scarcely understood, struck me like
a quivering arrow. In a whisper, I echoed, "Inoculation."

"Yes. But according to what little one has discovered
from testing on dogs, multiple inoculations are needed,
and they must be given before the victim begins to show
the symptoms of the dread disease."

"Oh," I said, again whispering, and then, because I
could not yet begin to comprehend what he was saying,
my floundering thoughts grabbed hold of something
I knew: what had brought me to Shellacker's Place in
Shoreditch in the first place.

I turned to look at this monumental man. In my normal tone I asked, "Dr. Lister, where do you get the dogs?
Where, specifically, did you get the black Alsatian?"

He froze, staring, as if I had accused him of some
crime.

I shook my head. "I am only trying to find out what
they did with my friend."

"Oh. Oh, dear." Now it was he whose voice dimin-
ished to a whisper. "I realise they are vigilantes of a sort,

taking the law into their own hands, but I cannot believe . . ." He bumbled into timid silence.

"The men with the mark of the ichneumon?" I pressed.

He nodded, his fluffy side-whiskers fluttering. "Ah, yes." He swallowed. "They brought me that particular dog; they bravely bring me many rabid dogs, trying to keep the streets safe for their women and children, you know, and—please do not think me morally remiss, but I simply do not question them."

I knew what he feared. I feared the same thing, and it was quite unspeakable, except by Mrs. Tupper. "They killed him right then and there," she had said.

I gentled my tone. "I think no such thing, Dr. Lister. Please, do you happen to know any of these intrepid men by name?"

"I—yes, a few . . ."

"And where they live?"

"I have locations where they have captured several dogs." He hesitated a moment longer, but then his head lifted in decision. "My records are in my office. Come with me."

He led me to yet another building, this one more

along the traditional lines of home and hearth, and by the time I left him, with many thanks and with a goodly amount of information written on a paper tucked into my glove, it was dark. Maud, carrying a lantern, showed me the way back to the hidden door in the Portland cement wall, through which she let me out. "Come back anytime," she invited, and I could not tell whether she was mocking me or she meant it.

Once outside the Portland cement wall, I simply stood there on an empty street in lamplight, feeling baffled by the strangeness of the place I had just left behind, reviewing in my mind the rabid dogs, the rabid rabbits, the dried brains, no-nonsense Maud, and earnest, humble Dr. Lister.

It was as if I needed to turn my back before I could face—his work—its enormity staggered my mind. "Oh, saints and martyrs," I murmured to myself, "he is trying to save the world from rabies."

• • •

I went quite without supper that evening, much to my vexation, as I had also missed breakfast, luncheon, tea, and dinner—but I felt I simply *must* report to Sherlock straightaway, and had not expected to find myself after dark in Shoreditch, a charmless place I knew not at all. More than once, as I walked at random in search of a cab, passing through crowds that seemed half drunk even on a Wednesday evening, I felt glad to have my dagger with me in my corset busk. By the time I finally found a cabstand, engaged transportation to the Shoreditch railway station, took the Underground back to London, and rode in another cab to Baker Street, my personage had given up nagging me for supper, instead nagging for sleep; it was past my bedtime. Indeed, it was so late that Mrs. Hudson knocked at my brother's door to make sure he was decent before she let me go upstairs to his flat.

"What on earth, Enola?" he greeted me rather crossly at the door, letting me in.

"Good evening to you, too," I retorted, but not harshly. A long day's growth of beard smudged the usually keen lines of his face, he wore a drab brown dressing-gown and carpet-slippers, and he looked tired.

I refrained from informing him I was equally tired, if not more so. *Have patience,* I chided myself mentally as I pushed a mess of newspapers to one end of the davenport for lack of a place to sit. "What on earth brings me here," I told my brother, "is some important new information on the Wolcott Balestier case." Gratefully lapsing onto the seat I had cleared myself, I turned to my brother. "I've tracked down and spoken with Mary Erasmus, and—"

And I was about to tell him all she had revealed about her pet vigilantes, then more of what I had learned from Dr. Lister regarding those same people—but I took a second look at Sherlock and paused to puzzle. Rather than settling down somewhere in my vicinity to listen, he was wandering, apparently at random, in the shadows of his dimly lit abode, his hands in his dressing-gown pockets.

"Why don't you sit down and smoke a pipe?" I asked quite sincerely.

He gave me a dry glance. "Is that an empirical question?"

Actually, I realised, it was! Why was he keeping away from me and—yes, hiding his hands in his pockets? I had seen them, briefly, when he had let me in, and had noticed in passing something quite odd.

I sat up straight. "Sherlock," I demanded, "why on

earth, in your dressing-gown and in the privacy of your own home, are you wearing gloves?"

He ceased his aimless strolling to turn and glower at me. "Surely that is my own business," he complained, pulling his hands out of his pockets and displaying them in a kind of defiance. He wore rather seedy white cotton gloves, and on one of them I saw a slight streak of pink. "As it so happens, I find it necessary to treat my skin for a minor inflammation—"

"Horsefeathers!" I interrupted, jumping to my feet and striding over to him for a closer look at the stain on one of his gloved hands; then I looked him in the face, my heart swelling with pride for him, my peerless brother.

"The Mark of the Ichneumon!" I cried, beaming at him.

His jaw dropped, adding to my glee; it was always a delight to surprise a reaction out of him.

"Let me see." I actually grasped his hand and stripped the glove off of it; he did nothing to stop me. The shallow, vertical wound on the back of his hand looked nasty and quite new, pink and oozing, not yet crusted over with a scab. "They initiated you just tonight?"

His mouth, now closed, smiled slightly. "They initiated one Horace Tedder, dustman, just tonight."

"This estimable personage being you in disguise?"

Evidently so, and rather than honouring such a simple-minded question with an answer, he demanded, "Enola, how do you know of these people?"

"Observation, deduction, and talking with Mary Erasmus." I gave his glove back to him and returned to my seat. "It was she who gave them that preposterous name. Have you met her?"

"No, I've not yet had the honour." Sherlock seated himself also, on the other end of the davenport from me, sweeping the newspapers to the floor.

"You will find her remarkable. She is besotted by her own vocabulary."

"Evidently. But why the deuce a mongoose, Egyptian or otherwise?"

"Guardian animal."

"For the self-styled guardians of the street. I see."

I leaned towards Sherlock. "Have you yet found out what they have done with Cotswold?"

He rolled his eyes. "If you mean Wolcott Balestier, no, not yet."

"Mary Erasmus says they are holding him for safety, whatever in the world that means."

With a troubled look, Sherlock pulled off his other glove and twisted the pair of them together as if he might wring some truth out of them. "I think it means that they cannot make up their simple minds what to do with him. Perhaps some want to kill him, as was done in old times. Perhaps others are still deciding what to decide. All I know for sure is that they are terrified of rabies and determined to be heroes. Enola, I have barely scratched the surface of their so-called brotherhood."

"Do you know their names, or where they live?"

"No. They do not yet trust me so far."

I pulled out of my glove the paper I had tucked in there, on which was written the information Dr. Lister had given me. "The names of the ones who captured the black Alsatian and turned it over to Dr. Lister are—"

I frowned at the paper, trying to make out the words in dim gas-lamp light.

"The ones who *what*?" Sherlock sounded quite peevish.

"Never mind." In that moment I felt far too enervated to attempt to explain to him my logic, or lack thereof, in having traced the mad dog. "I have obtained a few names of these manly followers of the mongoose for you." Rising to go home, I handed them over to him, having already memorised them for my own sake: Freddy Finley, Dick Nicholas, Menelaus Young, Stumpy Matthews.

"Obtained *how*?" Sherlock demanded, but I barely heard him, for clocks started striking the hour all over London, bells gonging in church towers, Mrs. Hudson's cuckoo downstairs giving voice, Big Ben distantly bellowing.

Already it was early in the morning of Thursday. On Thursday evening of the week before, "Cotswold" had gone missing. He had been gone far too long, hopes of finding him grew smaller by the minute, and I felt desperately tired.

"I'm going home," I told Sherlock. "Good night."

Chapter the Twelfth

It was not a good night, and I slept badly. Shortly after dawn I gave up on slumber, rang for a tray, and breakfasted without much appetite despite the fact that I had missed breakfast, elevenses, dinner, tea, and supper the day before. When the maid returned for the tray, I asked her to have a boy sent to secure Harold and his cab, if possible. Then, after very necessary ablutions, I dressed in one of my plainer frocks, put on one of my less-bedecked hats, grabbed my humble reticule in lieu of a parasol (a lady must always be carrying something), and set forth.

"Good morning, Miss Enola," Harold greeted me. He stood on the pavement beside the cab, unloading my drawing kit, folding stool, et cetera, about which I had completely forgotten. "I trust you're well?"

This was his veiled way of asking what had happened yesterday after he had deposited me at the Underground. I ignored it. "And a very good morning to you, too, Harold," I said cordially.

"Just leave those things at the front door, would you, and knock? I very much thank you for the favour of taking charge of them."

After this was done, I instructed him to take me to Maiden Lane.

I had awoken with my brain in a considerable muddle as to what to do next, then decided to visit Miss Balestier. I had news to report to her, but more urgently I needed to feel that I had accomplished something.

"Perhaps I'd better wait, Miss Enola," said Harold when we arrived, as I descended to the pavement. In case I was turned away because it was so early, he meant. Surely that was what he meant.

"Very well," I replied a bit sourly, as if he were a chaperone.

But in fact I felt glad to know he was near when the parlour-maid opened the door, for her face looked mutinous when she saw me. "Miss Balestier is breakfasting," she said most disagreeably.

Her tone made me clench my teeth. Dismissing Harold with a wave, I stepped past her, necessarily pushing her inside, and took a seat indoors. "Kindly tell Miss Balestier I await her convenience."

"Yer card," she demanded not kindly at all.

"I could give you several calling cards, each with a different name on it. I feel quite certain your descriptive powers will enable you to inform Miss Balestier that I am here."

My adversary flounced away, and I mentally invoked the virtues of patience, expecting a long wait. But, to my pleasure and surprise, Miss Balestier appeared after only a minute, with a napkin still in her hand, wiping her mouth. She wore black, as before, but not silk, just a simple cotton frock and shawl. "Hello," she said, tossing the napkin onto a whatnot table. "Shall we go into the library?" An English woman of her class would have taken twice as many words, and some chitchat, to convey as much. Perhaps Americans were less formal?

Or perhaps she was not particularly delighted to see me?

"I'm sorry to interrupt," I said, remaining seated. "Won't you finish your meal? I—"

I meant to say I would be glad to wait, but she interrupted with some force, "Eating does not interest me these days. Come. Bernice," she called to a maid, "light the lamps in the library."

This was well thought of, for the room was windowless, consisting of bookshelves, Wolcott Balestier's desk, a small Turkish carpet, and two comfortable chairs.

Sitting in one of these, Caroline Balestier urged me, "Tell me everything."

"I will do so." I set aside my shawl and reticule before seating myself. "I apologise for visiting so early in hope of finding you at home."

"But I am not going out to show Wolcott's likeness to people anymore, not since you have told me he has been kidnapped. Please, speak!" She leaned so far towards me, in her urgency, that she nearly tipped her chair. "You have learned more?"

"A little. The group that is holding your brother captive—and this is, you must remember, only my best-informed belief—the group consists of common labourers endeavoring to keep the neighbourhood around Smutty Lane safe for their families. They call themselves the Mark of the Ichneumon."

I have seldom seen eyebrows rise so high or a face show such a degree of astonishment and disbelief. "They—they call themselves *what*?"

"The Mark of the Ichneumon. I know it is quite absurd, but the first part of it I can account for; they initiate new members by inflicting a mark upon the skin of their hands, thus." I stripped the gloves off of my own hands and demonstrated until I had scored a pink mark on the back of my right hand with the thumbnail of the left. "They do it until they draw blood."

Carrie Balestier's brows arched to their utmost. "How—how grotesque!"

"Yes."

"That is the mark, then, but—an *ichneumon*? I am not sure I even know what that is."

"An Egyptian mongoose."

"They *have* one?"

I felt diverted by the idea; how amusing it would be if they had an actual, living mongoose! But I remained professional in my manner. "That I can't say. The moniker was given by an extraordinary woman of a certain age who appears to be their leader."

"A woman! Their leader? But how . . . why . . ." The idea flabbergasted her. Obviously she was not a Suffragist, nor had she ever met my mother.

I said nothing except, "I do not yet know much about her. She seems to be a working-class woman, modestly dressed, yet she exhibits learning and vocabulary one would not expect from her. She explains the ichneumon as an Egyptian guardian animal, defender against crocodiles, a fitting symbol for those who guard the safety of the streets."

Miss Balestier's face quite changed expression, turning somber and shadowed. "And what are these so-called guardians of the streets doing with my brother?"

I could only make a helpless, questioning gesture with my hands. I did not, could not, would not tell her they might kill him.

She frowned. "Does Mr. Holmes know of these people?"

"Yes, of course! He is actively investigating them."

"And you?"

In truth, I did not know what more I could do, but I hedged. "I have found out that there is a local source for the inoculation that could save your brother from rabies."

"If he can be found!"

"He shall be found."

"But—I wait at home, and minutes pass like hours. What can I do for Wolcott? Is there anything I can do?"

Her heartfelt plea impelled me to think of some task, however trivial, for her. "You could find the other witness who saw the mad dog bite your brother," I hazarded. "She is one of General Booth's soldiers in his Salvation Army."

"I shall inquire at their headquarters, and on the streets if I must!" Carrie's face glowed with purpose. "What is her name?"

"Agatha Bellwether, she said. But she may have dissembled, so wait a moment." I got up, fetched from the shelves one of the numerous books that surrounded us, reached into my reticule for paper and pencil, then resumed my seat. With the paper on the book in my lap, I drew the face of the "Hallelujah Lassie" with her close-set eyes, unlovely nose, and her ponderous jaw cradled by a great bow of black ribbon securing an old-fashioned black straw bonnet—

Caroline Balestier, watching me sketch, exclaimed, "I know who you are—the younger sister of Mr. Holmes! Ruddy told me about you!"

I paused my pencil to look up at her with a smile. "Mr. Kipling had nothing very kind to say about me, I'm sure."

"He told me you have a marvelous talent for capturing people's faces on paper, that's all. And now, looking at you, I can see how much you resemble your brother. But you told me you had no association with Mr. Holmes!"

Wryly I said, "At the time, I didn't." Quicky finishing my drawing, I stood to hand it to her. "If you can find this woman and coax her to tell you truthfully all she knows about the Mark of the Ichneumon, the incident of the mad dog, and your brother, you will have done a great service."

"But when shall I see you again?"

"I can't say. Any information you bring to light, you should convey directly to Mr. Holmes. Farewell, and good hunting." I made for the door.

"Miss Holmes, wait!" Caroline Balestier cried. "I still do not know your given name!"

I answered only with a mischievous grin as I hastened away.

• • •

Enduring the cab ride on the way home—hansoms are not always pleasant; mud spatters one's skirt, stray sheets of newspaper fly into one's face, and the wind threatens to take one's hat off—but disregarding these minor discomforts, I pondered the paradox that was Rudyard Kipling. He had told Miss Balestier that I drew well, but only that? This seemed odd, quite odd, as, to the best of my knowledge, he heartily disliked me.

Perhaps Carrie Balestier had prevaricated? Or perhaps Rudyard Kipling was playing at a game of some sort regarding me?

By the time I reached the Professional Women's Club, I had decided to find out.

Elevenses were just being served as I entered, and I sat down at the breakfast room table and devoured a great deal of soup and biscuits, for I would most likely miss luncheon. Then I excused myself and dashed upstairs to my lodging, where I threw open the doors of my wardrobe, feeling challenged as never before to wear something daring.

After a moment's thought, I pulled the bell-cord, for I was going to require the assistance of a maid. One cannot very effectively bind one's bosom by oneself.

And after another moment's thought, I opened my door to see whether any of my neighbours were about, for I was likely to require more assistance than just the maid. Smiling, I pursed my lips and started to whistle the minstrel's song from the *Mikado*. Before I was even a quarter of the way into it, other doors opened, heads peeked out, and several women appeared from downstairs, presumably having heard me and wondering what was going on, for whistling ladies were not generally approved of. "A crooning cow, a crowing hen, and a whistling woman earn bad ends," said the proverb.

Pish the proverb. I left off whistling and spoke. "A wand'ring woman, I, have met a certain gentleman I cannot please. He has disliked me in simple, scholarly garb, and in my most elegant visiting costume, and yet again in a wondersome ball gown—"

"We quite remember the ball gown," my elderly neighbour put in, and we all laughed.

"Forsooth, he detested me in all of the above," I continued, "so I have decided to call on him today, if you will ever so kindly assist me, dressed up as a man."

"Oh, my goodness gracious," said the phrenologist, with round eyes and great solemnity, "is that going to please him any better?"

"Most likely not. I intend to go as Oscar Wilde."

Thereafter ensued a merry uproar. We all loved Oscar Wilde, his plays, his poetry, and his style. Whilst the prevalent English fashion colour was black (due to Queen Victoria's interminable mourning), Oscar Wilde outfitted himself most colourfully in more ways than one, standing flamboyantly anti-fashion; how could we not adore him? At one of the fancy-dress parties we enjoyed monthly at our Club, six of him had showed up at once! (Six of us got up as him, that is.) Therefore, the items I needed were available in abundance. My friends scattered to collect costume sundries whilst the maid assisted me with bosom suppression; there would be no corset for me today, and shockingly little by way of underpinnings, only swaddling and a pair of knickers.

Scarcely were those in place when a dozen women swarmed into my room carrying Oscar Wilde's characteristic Bohemian trappings: broad-brimmed hats, frilled or ruffled silk shirts, braid-trimmed waistcoats, knee-breeches with bows at the sides, white stockings, pumps instead of boots, and of course, the utterly necessary cloaks he wore always and with greatest panache.

Given the necessity that the knee-breeches and waistcoat must fit me properly, I ended up with no choice but burgundy red velvet ones, and after that all else followed: an ecru wide-collared shirt, a flowing cerulean ascot, a pair of rakish, deep-cuffed raspberry-pink gloves, and a purple cape. Part of my hair hung down in spirals, courtesy of curling-irons most obligingly heated by the cooks in the kitchen. The rest of my tresses were pinned up to hide under my hat (a dark blue one, quite plain compared to the headgear I was accustomed to wearing). The final effect, I was told repeatedly by all involved, was perfectly aesthetic and "Neronian," a tribute to the hedonism of ancient Rome. I exited the Professional Women's Club amidst applause and cheers.

Directly outside, Harold and his cab awaited me, and as usual he maintained an expression on his face as bland as that of his horse, Brownie. For this I was grateful. "Where to, Miss Enola?" he asked.

"To 43 Villiers Street, Charing Cross." I could have saved a great deal of money by taking the railway rather than a cab, but I did not quite dare. Apparently, there were limits to my stomach for public effrontery. Thank heavens for Harold.

Villiers Street, seen again, turned out to be a very built-up, narrow snip of road leading from the Strand to the Embankment. Kipling's address commanded a view of the Thames, Waterloo Bridge and the shot tower and docks and stench and all, including hooting steam-tugs towing barges. Otherwise, it was without charm, having by way of ornament only railings in front of the upstairs windows for safety. As for downstairs, there was no proper entryway. I went in the front door and, as I was met by no attendant of any kind, I continued straight up the steep and shadowy steps to the first floor, where I scanned several doors, chose the one with its transom open for air (indicating occupancy), and knocked.

"Come in!" yelled a surly voice I recognised.

I went in, and saw him across the room from me, sitting in the light from a wide-open window to the street.

Intent on finishing the sentence he was scribbling on a block of writing paper, he did not yet look up at me, but two sizeable griffin heads snarled at me from the carved walnut arms of his Morris chair. Next to him on a library table stood several squat square bottles of ink in various colours—blue, black, crimson, violet, green—and extra fountain pens, and eyedroppers to fill them, and blotting paper, and a great many strewn sheets of scribbled or wadded paper. Still writing, he asked, "Who is it?"

"Enola Holmes," I said.

He dropped his pen; it fell to the floor and, as is the wont of fountain pens, spouted a puddle of ink. Unconcerned by this, Kipling gawked at me, snatched off his thick spectacles, fumbled for a different pair, then put them on and gawked some more.

"East is East and West is West," I explained. "I am female and you are not, and never the twain shall meet, so I thought perhaps we could stand face-to-face as two men, brave or otherwise."

"You mock me," he growled.

"Not at all. I was very much moved by your reading of 'The Ballad of East and West.' I quite desire to bypass border, breed, and birth or any other bumbleheaded barriers. So,

I chose to visit you, who are a man of letters, as Oscar Wilde, another such."

"Oscar Wilde is a mollycoddle," Kipling said, setting aside what he was writing and rising, with some difficulty, from his fully reclined Morris chair. His expression seemed huffy, but perhaps only because he was awkwardly exerting himself.

"Oscar Wilde is a renowned author," I countered, careful to maintain serenity of voice. "Do you not consider his poem 'The Harlot's House' as good as your own excellent verse? Very different, of course, but of similar literary value?"

"My poetry tells of valour and brotherhood in arms. Wilde's evokes a fey dismay." At least he seemed to be answering me seriously, and he motioned me towards a settee and armchair grouped on the other side of the room. I perched on the settee, and he came over and sat in the armchair facing me, giving me a grim look. "However, dismay seems quite in order, under the circumstances."

"Circumstances?"

"That indeed my beloved Wolcott Balestier, my very best friend, has been bitten by a mad dog!" The words burst out of him like gunfire, shaking him with a visible recoil. But, in a moment, as if taking a grip, he proceeded more quietly, "Or so Mr. Sherlock Holmes has informed me, citing evidence provided by you. He says you were right all along. Evidently I have wasted precious days by disbelieving you."

I was so astonished by this admission that I fear my face showed it, but luckily he did not see. He had lowered his eyes, not caring to look at me, and I thought it best not to speak.

"And the hell of it is," he went on, "those wasted days scarcely matter, because if you are right, then there can be no true rescue. The outlook could not possibly be much worse." His voice grew so low I could barely hear him. "Perhaps my friend, the best friend ever to brighten my life, is already dead. Or perhaps he is hiding to save us from himself, from the burden of his doom, because even if we find him, he must die."

"Nonsense," I said.

His head jerked up, and he certainly looked at me then, with rather the expression of one of the menacing griffins carved on his chair.

Hastily I added, "I mean, we must all die, eventually,

of course, but not necessarily of rabies. If only we can find Cotswold, we can take him to have an inoculation."

His griffin stare hardened.

I tried again. "Rather, several inoculations over a period of time, to be administered in the muscles of the midriff, for some reason, and therefore rather unpleasant and painful," I admitted, "but far preferable to hydrophobia."

Finally the griffin moved the stony mouth beneath its scrub-brush moustache, and spoke. "Are you talking about that charlatan in France?"

"No, I'm talking about someone right here in Shoreditch."

Kipling's jaw sagged, thereby becoming much less griffinish and more human.

"And he's not a charlatan," I added with some indignation. "Dr. Lister is—"

Quite well respected, I wanted to say, but evidently Kipling knew this. His eyes hugely widened, eclipsing his spectacles from behind. "Dr. Joseph Lister? He is working on a cure for rabies?"

"Not a cure, exactly," I quibbled. "Rather, a prevention." But then I had the good sense to give in. "Exactly. Yes."

Kipling became so fervidly interested, asking so many questions, that I ended up divulging a great deal about my encounter with the paradoxical Dr. Lister, an unpretentious man intent on conquering rabies. I described Shellacker's Place and some of what happened there, Lister's farming of rabid animals and his strange harvest, their dried brains. At one point whilst I was speaking, Kipling fetched me a glass of water. I drank it, then earnestly and clumsily explained how the dried spinal cords were powdered under the most sterile possible conditions and combined with sterile water to make inoculations.

"To be injected," said Ruddy as if still finding any of this difficult to believe.

"Yes."

"With a syringe. Like cocaine."

"I wouldn't know."

"No, of course you wouldn't." A strange look, both sad and smiling, wafted across his face and was gone. He leaned back in his armchair, seeming for the moment quite human. "Enola," he said, "may I call you Enola?" But he did not wait for an answer before continuing to do so. "It is quite absurd of me, Enola, but I actually do find it less fatiguing to talk with you when you appear to be a man."

"You are right," I told him pleasantly. "Quite absurd."

I do not think he exactly caught my meaning, because he continued to muse, "You are female, but if I face you as a man, even a dandy with ribbons on his knees, how very much more at ease I feel."

I looked down at my burgundy velvet breeches, which I had quite liked, ribbons and all, up until that moment. "That is too bad," I said, making sure to allow only sympathy to be heard in my voice. "But are there no women with whom you can so comfortably talk? Your mother?" His face froze, so I quickly spoke on. "Miss Caroline Balestier, for instance?"

He unfroze. "That is different. She is so much like her brother, full of lofty ideals and energy yet such quick sympathy, such delicacy of comprehension. . . ." His gaze shifted, and so, evidently, did his thoughts. "Cotswold was—is—a charming companion. Why, we were— are—writing a novel together, and I never thought I would ever share such intimacy of mind with any human being. I think I have never loved a man more."

He spoke with such frank intensity that he stunned me, and I retreated by asking a cowardly, commonplace question. "What is the name of the novel?"

"*The Naulahka*. It is about a fabled jewel of India."

"Ah." I glanced at the library table, the papers, the Morris chair. "Are you working on that today?"

"No. I was trying without much success to work on my own novel. . . . Enola, I am lost without Cotswold."

This time I caught myself before retreating. I took a deep breath to address, finally, the question I had come here to ask. "Mr. Kipling, have you any notion where he might be?"

He just looked at me.

Wondering exactly how much Sherlock had told him, I asked, "Of what do you think when I say the word 'ichneumon'?"

"Of an Egyptian mongoose, of course, and also of Darwin's fly. Why?"

Startled, I answered him only with another, sincere question. "Darwin's fly?"

"Darwin felt unable to believe in a creator because

there is too much misery in the world. He wrote, 'I cannot persuade myself that a beneficent and omnipotent
God would have designedly created the Ichneumonidae
with the express intention of their feeding within the
living bodies of caterpillars.'"

"Ichneumonidae?"

"I repeat, Darwin's fly. Actually, some sort of wasp,
I believe."

Out of my depth, I made a number of hasty mental
notes, then straggled back to my original question. "Mr.
Kipling," I said, "you know Wolcott Balestier far better
than I. You were, or are, writing a novel together. That
should give you some insights into his mind. Let me ask
you this: If I am entirely wrong about his being held
captive, if instead he is in hiding—then where would he
hide?"

Kipling did not need to take time to think, but responded at once with a tigerish grin. "In the jungle! Far
aloft, in the tippy-top of the tree growing from the tree
growing atop the very tallest tree!" The impetuous poet
I did not yet dare to call Ruddy surged up from his chair
to pace the room, which seemed not nearly large enough
to contain him. "Cotswold has no truckle with caves and

hidey-holes," he said, more to the furniture than to me. "His refuge is the heights." But then he turned upon me sharply. "In fact, it's mostly due to him that I have my protagonist living on the top floor, up seven flights of stairs, in *The Light That Failed*. He and his chums are quite free and easy in a big box room up there, so far aloft that no one cares to climb the stairs and bother them. But in consequence of its height, the stairwell is a shaft of darkness unto doom. The whitest paper flutters down, down, into shadow and out of sight. . . ." His voice trailed away. He stared at nothing I could see.

"Mr. Kipling," I said for no reason except to recall him.

He looked at me as if coming back from somewhere fearsome and far away.

Caught with nothing of essence to say, impulsively I asked, "Have you ever actually met Mr. Oscar Wilde?"

He peered at me quite strangely, but then he almost smiled. "No. Not I. Have you?"

"No. Nor have I ever met Mr. Wolcott Balestier. But I intend to do so at my very earliest convenience. Good-bye."

"Good-bye," he said in a puzzled way as I left him.

Chapter the Thirteenth

Nor was he the only puzzled one. Ours had been a very strange conversation, and as I traipsed down his stairway from his apartment, my thoughts quite literally gave me pause. Before opening the front door to go out into the sunshine, I stood with words vying in my mind. Thick new man, ichneumon, and now the Ichneumonidae? Thick new man a day?

Shaking my head, I exited 43 Villiers Street and walked to the more crowded pavements of the Strand, trying to think where I might consult a really excellent dictionary. But my mental efforts were continually interrupted by whispers wafting from the other pedestrians on the pavement.

". . . scandalous Bohemian!"

"Who ever does he purport to be, making a spectacle. . . ."

"'Ave a butcher!"

In excited girlish sibilants I heard, "Oscar Wilde! Is that really Oscar Wilde?"

"Is it truly?" squeaked another girlish voice. "Oh, I adore his poetry, and *The Happy Prince*!"

Eager to escape, with eyes cast heavenward, I hailed a cab and had the driver take me to the Subscription Library, that odd font of wisdom all inwardly girded in iron and steel, on St. James's Square.

Once inside, I found the fishhook-shaped librarian, his flossy hair trailing longer than ever, who directed me to the several volumes, or "fascicles" as he called them, of the *New English Dictionary on Historical Purposes*. The fascicles were, he explained with some excitement, in ongoing process of publication. Thanking him politely, I carried the one I needed to a table in order to pore over it.

Wanting paper and pencil to take notes, I reached towards my bosom but discovered I had none today.

So, necessarily, I simply memorised the following: the word "ichneumon" came from the Greek *ikhneuein* "to track or hunt," and it was applied to both the Egyptian mongoose and Darwin's fly because the former hunted crocodile eggs and the latter "quite unfairly" preyed on living creatures—the larvae and pupae of beetles, moths, butterflies—in which to inject its eggs which then produced its parasitic young. Once hatched, they voraciously ate their hosts from the inside out, rendering them helplessly catatonic and ultimately, dead. Quite dreadful, really.

In order to properly understand this horror, being the pencil-prone person I am, I sought out other references in which I found pictures: long larvae nearly encasing the body of a caterpillar, an ichneumon wasp emerging from a butterfly's chrysalis, and the remarkable "Darwin's fly" itself, an exaggerated and greatly recurved parody of a wasp. But these false wasps, I learned, did not sting; they were not so honest. Ichneumons were deceivers, parasites, troublemakers, even killers. . . .

In the steely air of that cast-iron library, I found myself staring, once again, at the glass-fronted case filled with Chinese "devil's work" globes carved from ivory, fanciful layer upon layer upon more layers covering a core of who knew what? And I found myself wondering about Mary Erasmus and how many layers of her there might be, and what lay within. Her boutonnieres—each a scavenged flower stiffened with wire, disguised with greenery, wrapped with scrap fabric, sewn together, pinned, altogether contrived—they seemed a possible extension of her personality. And her exhaustive vocabulary bespoke complexity of mind. Her brag, "I, myself, thought of that as the most apt of all possible names, you know!" gave me pause. The most apt of all possible names, "ichneumon"? Thick new man? Mongoose? Darwin's fly? Altogether a tricky word, and hardly one appealing to common working folk; how had they let Mary Erasmus foist it upon them? And those odd, odd marks on their hands. . . .

My brother Sherlock now bore such a mark. He was infiltrating the brethren of the street, trying to penetrate their mysteries and find Wolcott Balestier. A bold approach.

If I was not to get in his way, then my task, I now realised, must be to locate and spy upon Mary Erasmus.

But it was too late to find her at the morning flower market.

Yet, for Wolcott Balestier's sake, I could not possibly wait until tomorrow. Somehow, in this huge city, I must track her down today.

• • •

While it is quite true that my name, Enola, backwards spells "alone," and while my fervidly Suffragist mother had raised me to depend very much on myself, I had learned, over the past few years, how very helpful friends can be. With this in mind, I returned to the Professional Women's Club and sloughed off the personage of Oscar Wilde. Truly, I felt quite grateful to escape his fame, get out of his masculine folderol, fix my hair, put on a favourite juniper-green frock, and return to being my homely and eccentric self.

And as such, I made use of the constituent parts of the Oscar Wilde costume—the broad-brimmed hat, silk shirt, velvet breeches and waistcoat, stockings, pumps, cloak, gauntlet gloves, et cetera—that is to say, as I trotted throughout the Club to return each item to its owner, I jokingly asked every woman I encountered, "I yearn for occasion to wear my new Worth gown. Do you know of any fancy-dress events taking place this evening?"

In other words, if I were a boutonniere vendor, where would I go on this particular night to sell my wares?

I hoped, you see, to locate Mary Erasmus and spy upon her. I hoped to follow her home undetected, and then, when I knew where she lived, why, something helpful might follow.

I did not detail this inchoate plan to any of my friends, but they all knew I was up to mischief of some sort, and by tea-time the Club was abuzz with speculation and possibilities: the wealthy Desborough family would be hosting a coming-out ball for daughter Renee at Claridge's on Saturday; Lord and Lady Metcalfe had arranged an engagement extravaganza for their daughter Lisle and her fiancé, Sir William Torpenhow, at the Savoy the same night; another ball, for one Lily Armitage, was to take place at the Grosvenor on Friday, which was tomorrow; indeed many grand events were planned for the weekend, but for Wolcott Balestier's sake I could not wait so long to act! What, oh what celebration worthy of boutonnieres might be held this very night, a Thursday?

"A fancy-dress ball in celebration of the silver wedding anniversary of the Earl of Alvington and his wife," added the advice columnist as the profiteroles were being passed, "tonight, because it is the exact date, at their home along the Buckingham Palace Road."

Ah. I would start there!

Directly after finishing my tea, I began by sending my usual messenger, a street urchin avid for pennies, with a message for Harold—if Harold were to be found. If not, I must make do without him.

Then I retired to my room and prepared to costume myself for the venture, taking pains to put together dress, shawl, head covering, and boots that would help me blend in, first with other people on the street, and later with the darkness of the night. I chose clothing of unadorned black to suit both purposes, laying out a small black straw hat, black stockings, dark petticoats and a black frock, all of cotton, for silk would rustle and give me away. But first I donned a black corset, which I took care to lace none too tightly. Its real purpose was to serve as scabbard for my ubiquitous dagger and as storage for my supplies in case of whatever might chance:

biscuits, fortifying sweets, a candle stub and matches, a length of stout twine, a small mirror for looking behind me, wire for lock-picking, and other such oddments. Then I dressed, making sure to wear my oldest, most comfortable boots. Once ready, I pulled on thin black gloves, then slipped down the back stairs to a side street where, yes, my favourite cab-driver and his faithful nag, Brownie, were waiting.

"'Ello, Miss Enola," Harold greeted me, tipping his battered grey bowler hat my way.

"Hello, Harold!" I caressed Brownie's head. The evening light was kind to him and his master; both looked almost handsome. Seeing me dressed like a burglar, a spy, or perhaps even a sleuth, Harold gave me an expressively blank look, but of course he would never ask me what temerity I planned to undertake.

"To Buckingham Palace Road," I directed him, "and just drive along it until I tell you otherwise."

By the time we got there it was dark, but it wasn't difficult to tell which was the Earl of Alvington's mansion, brilliantly lit, with carriages forming a queue in front of it. Handsome older couples, men in top hats and richly gowned matrons glittering with diamonds, were handed down from their coaches by antiquely costumed footmen in white stockings and powdered wigs, who then provided an escort up broad marble stairs to a grand doorway. Indeed, I found myself peering into such a kaleidoscope of luxury that it quite nearly gave me a headache, and I did not see Mary Erasmus anywhere in it. But after Harold had driven well past, I had him turn around inconspicuously, using side streets, so that I could have another try from the opposite direction.

And this time, amidst all the dazzle, I spotted a familiar flat-faced, stout, and corseted figure on the pavement beneath a streetlamp, doing what appeared to be a brisk business in boutonnieres.

Once more letting Harold drive well past, I stopped him at a safe distance, paid him, and bade him good night.

"Miss Enola." He seemed oddly reluctant to go. "Will ye be safe?"

"Of course. I merely need to do a spot of spying regarding the boutonniere seller, Harold. She'll not murder me with a gardenia." Laughingly I sent him on his way.

I laughed. Ha. Ha ha.

. . .

After Harold had gone, I walked back along Buckingham Palace Road, keeping my pace neither brisk nor laggard, being just another person on the pavement, until I once more caught sight of my prey and her tray of boutonnieres. Then I drifted off to the side in search of a vantage point, which I found in the shadow of a pilaster flanking the side entrance of the stately manse next door to the Earl of Alvington's. There I stayed, watching Mary Erasmus and thinking about ichneumons in their various guises and who or what was this well-upholstered young woman, really?

I kept an eye on her for an hour or more, and grew stiff with stillness, standing behind that pilaster, before she finally gathered her posies into a bag and began to fold her tray. Whilst she bent to do this, I took the opportunity to leave the shelter of my pilaster and cross Buckingham Palace Road. By this time of night there was very little traffic, and I quite wished there were more, to hide me. I tried to walk in an utterly common, by-the-way manner across the cobblestones to the opposite pavement, which was not quite so much illuminated by the Earl of Alvington's splendour.

Mary Erasmus hoisted her accoutrements and walked away. I followed her at what I hoped was a safe distance, on the other side of the road, feeling very much like a bandalore swinging on the perilous end of its string in the hands of an inept fool. Only at this point, unfortunately, did it occur to me that I had never previously tried to "shadow" anyone on foot, and that there might be tricks to it I did not know. What if Mary Erasmus got a ride from a friend, or took the Underground, or boarded a train at Victoria Station, which lay only a few blocks away in the direction her nose was—"pointed" seemed hardly the word for such a flat facial feature—and I knew my thoughts were dithering; why had I not considered some of these possible misfortunes in advance?

Because it was useless. *Enola, you will do quite well on your own* said my mother's voice in my mind, calming me and reminding me to pay utmost attention. At every street corner I faced a crisis: Which way would Mary

Erasmus turn? For in London, there is never a straightforward route from anywhere to anywhere else. And at each turning, I lost sight of her for a little while before I dared to follow her, wincing every time my footsteps made a sound, for the streets were mostly silent except for the slow tread of constables patrolling their rounds.

My mind was not nearly so silent, bleating with trepidation every step of the way, but for a good two miles I followed Mary Erasmus without incident as she zigzagged her way north and east, utterly ignoring Victoria Station. Presently I could see the electric blaze of the Embankment lighting the sky, and that of the Savoy farther along, and I ventured to guess where we were going. Yes! Cobblestones ceased and streets narrowed to muddy lanes as we entered the poorer neighbourhood north of the Strand, the neighbourhood where I had sold tinware one day and posed as a plein air artist the next. My misgivings quieted, for I found myself once again on Smutty Lane! And this area was populous and noisy, even at midnight, with groups of drunken men and women gathered on pavement corners, whilst, in between, street urchins squabbled over orts of bread or huddled like puppies in doorways, trying to sleep.

It appeared Mary Erasmus was known in this area, for she exchanged greetings with loquacious drinkers or even stopped to talk with them. When she halted, I hung back and attempted to look utterly unremarkable, loitering near the inebriated so as to appear to be with them. Careful not to appear to watch Mary Erasmus at all, I kept her in sight, sometimes through a clump of people, sometimes as a reflexion in a shop window, and sometimes from the corner of my eye. At times when she moved on, I would tarry a bit so as not to be obvious, and then I would hurry like a dervish so as not to lose her. It was most awkward, especially as I did not want to be noticed, and I was very glad indeed when Mary Erasmus stopped at the shabby front door of a tall building of flats, produced a key to open it, then disappeared within.

A moment later, trying to appear deep in introspection, or perhaps retrospection, I ever so aimlessly strolled to that door to find out what was the number of the building.

But, immediately upon facing it, I forgot all about that errand, for on the door's faded wooden surface was limned, in what appeared to be shiny black paint, a large half-circular something that seemed to jeer at me, somehow. Uneasy, peering, at first I took it for a sort of deviant crescent moon with a nasty, lumpy tail trailing. Not until I noticed wispy wings painted with a skilled hand did I make it out: an insect with a long and very curved tail fastened by a tiny waist to a bump of torso and a bead of head. A wasp, flexed to sting.

An ichneumon wasp.

My jaw fairly sagged.

That this bizarre artwork signified the Mark of the Ichneumon I had no doubt. But who, among that workman membership, was aware of the double meaning of "ichneumon"? Who would have, or could have, painted—

Wait a minute.

Regaining control of my jaw, I bent to examine the rather vicious-looking picture more closely, then removed one of my gloves and touched it. Also, at that closer distance, I could smell it.

The "paint" was actually nail lacquer.

The ichneumon wasp on this door was, no doubt in my mind, put there by Mary Erasmus.

I straightened, slid my glove back on, and took a deep breath, staring at the obscurity of the shadowy night, mentally attempting to fathom the darkness within this woman. All the time she had preached of guardians, safety, and protection, she had known of duplicity, predation, and parasitism. Very likely she had known right from the start what had happened to Wolcott Balestier. What if it were *she* who had him in her clutches?

I needed to get into that house. I reached, seized the knob, and tried the door, but it was, of course, locked.

Might I enter by a window, perhaps? I scanned them, but by the meager illumination provided by streetlamps, I could tell very little.

And I got no farther than that, because something quite unexpected happened: my conscience smote me, reminding me that the case of this missing man, Wolcott Balestier, belonged to my brother Sherlock, not I. From what I had just discovered, Mary Erasmus might be the key to the whole mystery. Confound everything, I realised to my dismay, it was clearly, first and foremost, my duty to tell *Sherlock* about this most sinister woman and this equally sinister place. Straightaway.

It took me a moment to reconcile myself to this decision rather than blundering into the house on my own. But then, with a sigh of saintliness, I turned my nose (a much better pointer than that of Mary Erasmus) in the direction of Baker Street and strode off that way, brisk and brimful of virtue, to do my duty.

But, again, something quite unexpected happened. Alas.

Even before I reached the first corner, someone—a very strong someone—clapped his hand over my mouth from behind, and two other strong someones seized my arms.

Chapter the Fourteenth

My instant reaction, if I may say so, was either brilliant or insane: I propelled both feet with great decision towards the men on each side of me, letting the force of gravity take charge of my body. Due to this sudden plunge, the one who had my head nearly lost his grip, and all three of them exclaimed words so naughty I had never heard them before. However, regrettably, two more men appeared who managed to grip my ankles even though I thrashed and kicked. I bit the callused hand that covered my mouth; I sank my teeth into it as hard as I could. The man on the other end of the hand swore like a common labourer (which, indeed, is what they all proved to be), but he only tightened his grip, then wrapped his forearm hard around my head, covering my eyes. With that, my moment of glory was over; between the five of them they had me bang up to the elephant.

Lifting me by both arms and legs (and, by the way, my head), they carried me, with no more trouble than if I were a frisky lamb, in through a door and up several flights of stairs. They said nothing, and I could see nothing, but deduced what was happening from footsteps and grunts and the varying attitudes undertaken by my personage. Likewise, I could tell when they stopped climbing stairs, changed course, and entered a room through a door that squeaked on its hinges most plangently.

Need I say that I did not at all enjoy any of this? Evidently, Mary Erasmus had been slyly aware of my clumsy attempt to shadow her, and had, by talking to people on the street, set a trap for me. I felt utterly a fool as my captors stopped, dumped me, and my rump impacted a hard floor.

But even in my chagrin, I was ready to seize this chance. The instant their hands let go of me, before I could see much more than an eyeblink of my dimly lit surroundings—a gang of men in a dreadfully common room—I sprang to my feet and reached for the dagger sheathed in the busk of my corset, its hilt disguised as a rather tasteless brooch.

But I never touched it. My hand halted in midair, and my entire personage abruptly ceased to cooperate with me, all my impetus arrested by the sight of a face.

Not any of those nearest to me. The hard, hirsute men around me had already seized my hands and were tying them behind my back as I stood without resisting, barely noticing, gawking at the gentle, sensitive, suffering face of a gentleman who was seated on the floor and leaning against the wall opposite me. Shadowed by lamplight and misery, he looked back at me without any spark or spirit. He didn't know me, but I knew him. It was Wolcott Balestier!

But almost before I could gasp, my view of him was blocked. Mary Erasmus stepped in front of me, her head thrust forwards so that she presented to me, only inches away, a most unpleasant countenance. "Meddlesome shrew! Who are you?" she demanded with such force that I received an almost stupefying blast of her breath, which smelled of curried chicken livers.

I stepped back, snapping, "Xanthippe!"

Gentle reader, the historical Xanthippe was the wife of Socrates, who had said terribly disparaging things of her, so I said this to insult her—but apparently Mary Erasmus was not quite as much of a scholar as she thought. Seeming to take it as my name, she barked, "Xanthippe *what*?"

"Zan," I told her icily. "Thippy."

She blinked, then pressed on. "You are one bollock of a Nosy Nellie, that's what you are, with yer hair all in a mess."

Only then did I notice that in the fracas I had lost my hat, and my hair was coming down. "Oh, dear me," I said sarcastically.

"Dear you? Not 'ere! Whatcher been following me around for?"

"To find him." I nodded towards Balestier, who was observing me dully.

Mary's scanty eyebrows lifted, and she uttered a short, unpleasant laugh. "Well, you found him," she said, "and much good may it do you. Sit down on the floor." Quite roughly she "helped" me there with a shove. "Tie her feet," she ordered, turning to the five men standing around her—men with hobnailed boots and shabby clothes, un-shaven faces and dirty fingernails and yes, the Mark of the Ichneumon like a red burn on the back of their left hands.

I started to sort them out in my mind. The one who was binding my feet wore ragged gaiters from his knees to his ankles; I called him Gaiters. Another one was Gibface, because of his ugly mug with a thunderous huge jaw; he stood there nursing a bloody hand, so evidently he was the one I had bitten. A paltry victory, I thought, scanning the rest of the thugs. The paunchiest one I dubbed Tallowgut. The skinny one with baggy trousers held up by suspenders was Braces, and the remaining one I called Ratbag. They were all ratbags, actually.

Mary Erasmus glared inclusively at them. "Take care of Miss Know-It-All," she growled, jabbing a forefinger at me, "straightaway. No shilly-shallying."

"Who put you in charge?" one of the men grumbled just loudly enough to be heard but not identified.

Instantly she seemed to grow inches taller, and in the deep, commanding voice of a Ratbag-in-Chief she ordered, "Silence! Who put a roof over your good-for-nothing heads?"

"It's yer father's rotten diggings, not—"

But she ranted on as if she heard only insects. "Who gave you a worthy calling, you wastrels trying to be men? Whose was the grand scheme of the ichneumon? Who made you guardians against villains and rabid beasts? *Who?*"

Only mumbles answered her.

Commanding, "Do your duty, or you are not worthy of the mark on your hands!" she strode out of the room and slammed the door behind her.

Gibface spat on the floor. "That's a spoiled woman fer ye." But he kept his voice down.

"Just because 'er father was a whitesmith," grumbled Braces in the same muted tone.

"Look at 'er. She 'asn't missed many a supper, 'as she? Not like us," muttered Gaiters.

Then all five ratbags gave one another closed looks and, by some sort of tacit accord, shuffled to the other end of the room, where they started to converse in low voices, over whether and/or how to "take care of me," I had no doubt. Gibface seemed to be holding forth the most. Tallowgut sat down on the floor, and the rest of them stood; there were no chairs. Braces produced a bottle of whiskey from somewhere out of his voluminous trousers, and they started passing it around.

Bound hand and foot with business-like twine, I was left sitting in the middle of the floor facing Wolcott Balestier, or at least a grey, embodied ghost of the Balestier I had seen in photographs. This was a Cotswold with hollow cheeks and no puckish, eager glance for me. Deathly despair shadowed him, and no wonder, as he surely thought he was condemned to die from rabies, so what did it matter to him if ruffians killed him sooner? He could care about nothing else whilst the spectre of rabies haunted him.

I most urgently needed to rouse him. I needed to speak to him, but in such a way that our uncouth captors—thank goodness they were preoccupied by liquor—would not understand a word I said.

I thought.

Hmmm.

Aha!

Inspired, I leaned towards Wolcott Balestier and peered at him.

"Behold, Cotswold," I addressed him quietly, "thou most esteemed comrade of the great one who kipples—"

He sat up straight, his shadowy eyes widened, and he regarded me with startled attention.

"I bear glad tidings," I continued, warming to my self-imposed task of using oldish English combined with exalted vocabulary as a kind of secret code. "Thou wert most foully wounded by the unclean tusks of a canine," I said earnestly, "but thou needest no longer contemplate imminent mortality in consequence thereof! Mere hydrophobia need not doom thee! Thou hast recourse to medical salvation in the form of inoculation!"

He continued to gaze at me fixedly, rather like a puzzled scientist presented by a vermicular biological specimen and trying to decide whether it was worm or snake or legless lizard.

"I speak sooth," I told him with even warmer emphasis. "Verily, mere furlongs from here, physician Lister—knowest thou Lister, of carbolic acid fame? In his proximate stronghold, Lister doth abstract philtres of recondite substances gleaned from the brains of canus insanus—"

"Do you never speak normal English?" Cotswold interrupted me.

He sounded more appealing than irate, and at last

he had spoken! He had a pleasant tenor voice, well-modulated and cultured despite his American accent.

I am afraid I answered him a trifle sharply. "I am striving to communicate without arousing cognition among . . ." I tilted my head towards the five rough men I was watching from the corner of one eye. So far, they had given me a few curious glances, but seemed preoccupied by their tippling deliberations.

"Never fear cognition among that lot," said Cotswold with a hint of humour in his tone. "They know they are expected to kill me, but can't seem to make up their minds to accomplish it."

"Again, I bespeak thee, thou needest not die, neither from them nor from hydrophobia! It would behoove thee to flee, methinks." I gave him a long, earnest look.

"Methinks, also," he admitted with the ghost of a grin, "but whereby?"

"Dost spy the tasteless rubicund brooch I wear?"

"Aye, marry, I do." He smiled a bit wider, getting into the Shakespearean spirit. "Whatever thereof?"

"'Tis the hilt of my dagger."

His eyes goggled. He whispered, "Xanthippe, what sort of she-djinn are you?"

"The garden variety. Hearken thee, canst thou get thyself unbound?"

He opened his mouth to answer, but a voice from the far end of the room stopped him. It was Gibface, who grumbled loudly and decisively to his fellow ratbags, "Well, wot hever we do got ter wait fer nightfall." Then he stepped over to the oil lamp and blew down the chimney to put it out. Its flame vanished, yet light remained, and, blinking in astonishment, I realised it was dawn! Pale sunlight filtered into the room through grimy windows.

As if it were perfectly normal to settle down for sleep at dawn, Braces and Ratbag said "G'night" and departed. Tallowgut lumbered up from his seat on the floor, stretched, yawned, belched, then ambled toward some destination behind my back, where I could no longer see him, but I heard him halt—and then I heard a squirting sound rather like that of a cow being milked into a metal bucket.

Oh, horrors. Yes, most likely a metal bucket stood in the corner behind me, but what was going into it had nothing to do with milk.

The sound ceased, and presently Tallowgut reappeared, crossed to the other side of the room, and quite simply lay down on the floor, as there were no beds, nor even blankets. Gaiters, in his turn, approached the bucket behind my back, alas and wellaway! Stiff with revulsion at hearing what he was doing, I quite wished I could cover my ears, but my hands remained firmly bound behind me. Desperate to do *something* about my wretched situation, I turned to Gibface and told him loudly, "I'm hungry."

He jumped as if a piece of furniture had spoken to him, then leered at me in a most unattractive way. "There's nothin' to eat."

"Nothing to *eat*?" I echoed in feigned upper-class shock and disbelief. (Compared to theirs, my simple but intact clothing was upper-class.) "No bread?"

"No bread," he mimicked me nastily.

I felt a giddy impulse to follow Marie Antoinette's reasoning and ask for cake, but I repressed it.

"Why should *we* 'ave summat to eat?" Gibface went on. "We're common folk here."

Gaiters reappeared to stand beside Gibface, both of them starting to look amused as they watched my face, for I was doing my very best to appear stupidly peevish and dumbfounded, but meanwhile thinking furiously.

"Nothing to eat," I repeated as if this were incomprehensible to me, but then I rallied, glaring at them. "Well, might I at least use the loo?"

Their jaws all but dropped at my absurd assumption that there was a proper facility—even Tallowgut sat up to gawk at me—but then, as I hoped, thoughts of how I might react when I encountered "the loo" entered their simple minds and instantly became irresistible. Their eyes lit up; would I scream, or would I actually attempt to lift my skirts and sit upon the bucket, in which case surely it would fall over and I would be utterly humiliated? They exchanged a single ebullient glance, and then Gaiters came over and untied me, feet first, then my hands. Gibface folded his arms, ready to take in the show, and even Tallowgut stood up to watch.

I made sure to calm my breathing, keep my face indifferent, and take my time, getting up with only the slightest glance at Cotswold to make sure he was paying attention—he was—and rubbing my wrists—not that the bindings had chafed them, not really, through my gloves, but I needed time to think. Slowly I turned around. The corner, I saw, was partitioned off by a crude screen. So much the better. Ignoring the eager watchers, I walked without haste towards it, then behind it.

But even as my back disappeared from their view, I snatched my dagger, gripped it between my teeth, grabbed for the disgusting bucket, picked it up with both hands, turned towards the enemy and charged.

I hurtled out from behind the screen and leapt towards the three ratbags, flinging the contents of the bucket straight into Gibface's unlovely eyes—he howled and fell down—then reversing the now-empty bucket and smashing Gaiters, then Tallowgut, in the face with its bottom. As they tottered back, I dashed to Cotswold, who was quite ready for me, holding his hands out so I had no trouble slashing their bindings with my dagger. But there was no time for me to free his feet, for I heard stomping boots and fervid curses rapidly impending behind me. So I pressed the hilt of the dagger into Cotswold's hands, turned, and charged—just in time. Ducking beneath outstretched hands, I managed to head-butt Tallowgut quite satisfactorily; with an "Oof!" he collapsed.

But the next moment, as I straightened, rough hands

grabbed my arm almost hard enough to break it off. I knew the feel of that clutch all too well; it was Gibface. I spun and drove the fingers of my free hand straight into both his poor dear eyes. With a most satisfactory howl he let go of me and staggered back, but the other one, Gaiters, grasped my shoulder from behind—

"Let her go," said a quiet, reasonable voice, and the rough grip slackened. I twisted free and turned to find Wolcott Balestier holding a dagger to the ratbag's throat. But Gaiters, still on his feet, looked more formidable than frightened; therefore, I aimed a hard kick at his knee to disable him. He must have moved, however, for I missed his knee and, instead, the point of my boot struck him directly between his legs. He gave a truly appalling scream, bent double, and fell.

I wondered what was the matter with him, but there was no time to investigate; Cotswold and I must flee. "Run!" I cried, taking his arm and urging him towards the door.

But he could not seem to run. He tottered beside me manfully, and we got through the door, but the moment we closed it behind us, he sank to the floor.

"Get up!" I cried, still clinging to the stupid idea that I could somehow whisk him away down flight after flight of stairs.

"Hardly." He rolled partway over to face me, his back wedged against the door, and he handed my dagger back to me. "My leg is useless. You run. Go! Now!" he commanded most urgently, for from the far side of the door sounded the most frightening curses, along with the scrape and thump of hobnailed boots.

Only because I knew I must find help for him, I ran. With my thoughts and, no doubt, my face in the greatest disorder, I bolted down the stairs at breakneck speed—and that is no mere figure of speech. I was truly in danger of breaking my neck, for there was no handrail, let alone a banister to slide down, and the steps were of the lowest order, rude rickety planks of wood without risers—one could see chasms of air between them, reminding one that it would be quite possible to slip and plunge quite a distance to the ground floor. I tried, at first, to take the steps two at a time (sheerest madness when descending), but one rotted wooden tread actually broke beneath the impact of my foot, and for a horrible instant I thought my life was over. But, falling, I managed to snatch at the next lower step and cling to it, swinging like a most unfortunate bell. Strengthened by terror, I pulled myself up to lie, perilously balanced, on my midsection.

Above the sounds of my heart pounding and my panting breath, I heard the most alarming ruckus from above—bashing and battering noises, fulsomely shouted curses, and Gibface's horrid voice roaring, after a fearsome oath, "All together now, we'll bust the blasted thing down!"

Then I realised Cotswold remained lying where I had left him, blocking the door for me!

Chapter the Fifteenth

I must get away, get help, save him.

With greatest haste and not much memory of how I managed, I climbed out of my predicament, got to my feet, and hastened down too many flights of stairs—what was it Ruddy had said about seven frightening flights of stairs—and before I reached the bottom, I heard a crash and a bang and the thunder of hobnailed boots not nearly far enough above me. The ratbags had breached the door and were hot on the chase after me.

Leaping down the last rickety stairway, I nearly fell,

but caught myself between narrow walls and dashed to the front door. The door with the mark of the ichneumon *wasp* on it, the door to the street! What if it were locked? But it was morning, and for the sake of labourers and daily women going to work, the door was merely on the latch. I flung it wide and burst out, onto the street, like a partridge breaking cover. Folk's sleepy eyes roused to stare at me as if I were a very strange bird indeed. With my hair fallen in a mess on my shoulders, I realised, I looked like a madwoman, and I am sure I acted like one, too, spinning to look about me, for I needed to find a hiding place, quickly, before my brutish pursuers caught sight of me.

I dashed to a drainpipe directly beside the doorway from which I had just emerged, and climbed for my life. The folk on the street gawked at me, but then hastened on; they dared not be late for work. Also, a nearby elevated train provided a noisy and welcome distraction as I reached the rather pitiful pediment above the door and huddled upon the peak of it.

At that very moment, as I looked down from directly above their heads, Gibface and Gaiters slammed out of

the building and ran into the street. Tallowgut, I deduced, had stayed behind to tie up Wolcott Balestier—
nothing worse, I prayed.

The other two glared up and down Smutty Lane
this way and that, both of them crouching and panting
like rat terriers ready to spring. "She gotter be near at
hand!" Gibface bellowed, then dashed off in an attempt
to discover me around the next corner; Gaiters ran in the
opposite direction.

I dropped from my perch to the pavement; if they had
turned to look behind them, they would have seen me. I
hurtled directly across the street, dodging carts and bar-
rows, towards another tenement like the one I had just
left. The sleepy drudges who lodged there were leaving for
work, meaning that the front door was open. I slipped in.

Forthwith, once inside the narrow, dark hallway, I
turned to the first flat on the left—the flat that had a
window necessary to my purposes, overlooking the street.
Imperiously I pounded on the door, but discovered at
once that the commotion inside me would not let me wait
for a response; I flung the door open and strode in.

The window was already occupied by three nearly
identical boys, all shock-headed, shabby, skinny, and

barefoot. One was tall (although not as tall as I), one small, and one in between. Brothers, I surmised, and they apparently lived here, as I saw a jumble of rags by way of bedding in each of three corners.

"Look here," I told them as they did, indeed, take a look, jumping to turn around and gawk at me. "I need your help."

To my astonished pleasure, they rallied like young soldiers.

"Yes, ma'am!"

"Yes, miss!"

"Yes, lydy!"

They must have seen me darting across the street in their direction, I realised, and likewise they must have observed my escape, evidently with approval.

The tallest, and presumably oldest, ran to bolt the door, declaring, "We'll hide you from them hooligans, miss!"

"I thank you for that. But they are worse than hooligans." Crossing the small, meagre room, I sat myself with a plop on the floor beneath the window, positioned so that I could peer over the sill. That way, I might go unnoticed, with only my eyes and the top of my head visible from Smutty Lane.

"They are kidnappers," I declared. "They are holding a man prisoner on the top floor."

I heard the boys, immediately behind me and also looking out of the window, gasp and murmur with dismay.

"A frail, starving gentleman," I elaborated. "I was trying to rescue him, but I failed. The ratbag with the monstrous melon of a belly is guarding him right now. I am watching to see what happens next, but suppose he takes him out by a back way?"

"I'll watch," declared the tallest tousle-head gallantly. My mind dubbed him Sir Stringbean, for he resembled one. Without waiting for me to say a word in reply, he dashed out, calling over his shoulder, "Bolt the door behind me!"

The remaining two boys did so as he ran across the street—I saw him—directly past Gibface and Gaiters, who were just returning from trying to chase me down. Having failed to do so, and obviously in ill temper, they met in front of the ichneumon-wasp door, gesticulating wildly as they exchanged a few unkind words before going inside.

The instant they did so, I stripped off my gloves

(horribly sullied now), cast them aside, and began min-ing my bosom, pulling out paper and pencil, shillings and pence, and lemon drops—I immediately gave one of the hard sweets to each of the remaining two boys, saying, "I shall need you to take messages for me."

Eyeing the money, they jammed the treats into their mouths whilst nodding with enthusiasm.

Laying my paper on the none-too-smooth wooden floor, I wrote a few words, trying to keep one eye on my message and the other on the enemy's door. This proved, of course, to be impossible.

"We'll watch fer yer, ma'am," offered the middle-sized boy, and he stood beside my shoulder to do so.

Still, I wrote my messages as quickly and briefly as possible:

Wolcott Balestier held captive Smutty Lane behind Savoy.
Come at once! Enola

Duplicating this on a second sheet of paper, I folded both, wrote names and addresses on the outside in coarse-hand, and, the instant my task was done, popped my head up to peer out of the bottom of the window again. Seeing nothing amiss, I handed the two messages to the two boys. "Can you read where they have to go?" I asked in some alarm; what if they couldn't?

"Yes, lydy."

"Read them aloud to me," I demanded.

They did so. The younger one faltered a bit, but managed.

"Good." I turned away from the window for a moment to face them with utmost sincerity. "Do you promise me, cross your hearts, to deliver these at top speed? I will pay you handsomely."

"We promise," said the older, and "Cross my heart," said the younger, and he did so.

"Go now," I ordered. "Run. Godspeed!" I called after them as they dashed out the door, but already I had resumed my cautious vigil at the window. With my eyes barely above the windowsill, I watched my messengers pelt down the street and disappear around the corner. At least they seemed to be heading in the right direction, but I all but whimpered with anxiety: Would they really, truly manage to deliver the messages, and quickly? By the looks of them they were consummate street urchins, well able to leap upon all manner of vehicles for a ride, and duck the buffets of those who attempted to dislodge them, and inquire among their rapscallion peers to find their way anywhere in London. I had done the best I could, enlisting their help, but what if they failed?

And what if Sherlock was not at home? And what if Gibface, Gaiters, and Tallowgut were doing terrible things to Cotswold? And what if they took him out the back way; could my tall tousle-head alert me in time? And even if so, what could I do? And if, and what, and more ifs, and there I sat clawing my skirt and peering surreptitiously out of a grimy window; was that really all I could do?

Yes, it really was, until aid of some sort arrived, but I found the wait almost unbearable; truly I wanted to cry and suck my thumb. Instead, I stuffed my mouth with lemon drops and hoped they would give me strength. I watched and watched Smutty Lane. Amongst other traffic, a blind man passed with a child leading him by the hand, a woman driving a donkey cart full of live chickens went by, many shabby folk trudged this way and that, but no one likely to render me aid. Not even a constable appeared, although just about anything else did: a scrawny stray dog trotting along as if it knew where it was going, a country gent on foot driving three unruly black-and-white-spotted calves, old women wearing shawls and carrying shopping baskets, a load of heavy cast-iron gateways drawn by a yoke of oxen, two disreputable-looking men—

Recognition struck me with such a jolt of shock that I nearly squawked out loud: I knew them. They were Ratbag and Braces, all the more unmistakable because (having slept in them?) they still wore the same clothes they'd had on before.

Numb with dismay, I watched them amble to the house I hoped they weren't heading for—but they were. Letting themselves in at the lacquer-painted door, they closed it behind themselves, and then—I felt quite certain, even though I could no longer see them—they climbed the very rudimentary stairs to join their fellows.

I felt quite sick with dread. As soon as they got to the top of those stairs, something horrible was going to happen. I quite simply knew this; I did not require my famous brother's deductive reasoning to know it. The men with the ridiculous mark of the ichneumon on their hands were going to "take care of" Wolcott Balestier.

My mind gibbered, knowing there was nothing I

could possibly do for Cotswold against so many enemies; nevertheless, my body sent me springing to my feet and running for the door. It was simply not physically possible for me to sit any longer on the floor, motionless and watching.

I pelted out of the pitiful flat, out of the tenement itself, and ran headlong into the street, trying to cross it whilst evading an old-clothes man, various wagons, an apparently demented youth on an enormous velocipede, a very muscular milkmaid barely stooped by the weight of her wooden yoke and its two huge dangling covered buckets—

A milkmaid with her hair cropped defiantly short around her plain, blunt face.

"Maud!" I yelled at her, and with no time for surprise, pleasure, or niceties, in the middle of the mucky thoroughfare I seized her by the arm, stopping her. "Help me!"

She stood like a post and gawked at me pop-eyed, but managed to speak: "Enoler?"

"Yes, Maud, please help!"

In a droll tone she asked, "'Ave ye lost yer pretty pink gloves?"

I wanted to shake her, but restrained my ungloved hands from doing so. Also, I managed to remain courteous. "No, but something has happened, Maud, and it concerns Dr. Lister." This was remotely true. "Will you help me?

"'Elp yer do what?"

I was spared trying to answer, for just then, "Miss! Ma'am! Lydy!" yelled another voice in close proximity, startling me as much as I had startled Maud. I turned to see Stringbean run up to me, panting. "They're taking him out the back!"

"We must stop them!" I screamed, whirling to run towards—I hardly knew where, but Stringbean, sprinting ahead of me, darted into a narrow sort of walkway, dark as a tunnel, between tenement buildings. I followed close on his heels, and within a few strides we emerged into daylight enough to behold a desolation of debris, rubbish all over the ground. The tenement house's cramped backyard was a fenced-in maze of wash-lines, rows of unlovely privies, hogsheads, woodsheds—but, glancing over the top of the fence nearly as tall as I was, I did not take in every detail, because my attention was riveted upon the scene at the back door: my five most detested adversaries hauling Wolcott Balestier down the stoop like a log of wood. I saw that he was bound hand and foot, he had a rag stuffed into his mouth, and his face was mottled with bruises—they had beaten him!

Fury took over any sensible faculties that remained in me, and I charged like the Light Brigade. I tried to vault the fence, found that in my accursed skirt I could not, and dashed towards the back gate instead, shoving Stringbean out of my way—he was already leaving anyhow, like a sensible lad. Dagger already in hand, I stood on one foot and kicked the heel of the other straight and hard into the latch of the gate; blessedly, the wood surrounding it caved in, and the gate swung open with a crash.

Startled, my five foes dropped Cotswold, but even as they turned towards me, I darted in, not stabbing but cutting, quick, quick, quick, any part of their anatomies within my reach. Circling to draw them away from where Cotswold lay, I got Tallowgut across his excess frontage, of course, and Ratbag on the shoulder, and Gibface across the forehead; he howled and staggered back, blood in his eyes. All the rest of them grabbed for me, bellowing curses, which reminded me to scream and keep screaming; it was most necessary that I should scream so that those who were coming to help—I hoped!—could hear me and locate me. Shrieking, with frenzied speed I slashed at the hands that were trying to seize me—but there were too many, it was like fighting an octopus; Gaiters got hold of my arm—

And a large cudgel of some sort clouted his head, laying him flat.

"Maud!" I cried, most unnecessarily, as she was busy fighting. Hefting her clumsy weapon, her wooden yoke, with both hands, she swung it like a mace, bashing Braces and sending Tallowgut and Ratbag scrambling for cover behind a hogshead—but at the same time, alas, something bashed *me*. Something that felt like a mallet hit my head instead of a croquet ball. I staggered back, dizzily identifying my attacker as Gibface armed with a piece of railing, and I made a rather sorry attempt to stab him; I missed. The next instant I found myself entangled in the legs of a long and disgusting laundry item hanging from one of the wash-lines. I could not get my arms free, could not use my dagger, and right in front of me appeared Gibface, his face frightfully twisted with hate, his stick raised to wallop me again. I kicked him somewhere in his midsection hard enough to make him drop the stick, but then he bellowed curses, bared his brown teeth in a snarl, and his big callused hands shot out to grab me. Unable to slash him or get away, I screamed in utmost earnest, so sincerely frightened that everything seemed to go unpleasantly white—

Except at that instant I saw, like a godling silhouetted in the whiteness, a broad-shouldered man vaulting towards me over the fence. In that fraught moment he looked dazzling to me, like a great raptor on the wing in a silver sky, an eagle stooping to strike. As I blinked, he landed, sprang, and attacked my assailant with a roar worthy of a tiger. Grasping Gibface by the shoulders, he actually lifted him off his feet and flung him bodily into a privy! Only when he whirled to do the same to Tallowgut did I take in his pugnacious face and recognise him by his bristling moustache.

"Ruddy!" I cried, exultant—quite irrationally so, as I was the one who had sent a messenger to summon him.

His hair flew wildly, for his hat had fallen off. Charging towards Tallowgut in a rage, he seemed not to hear me, which was just as well, for I should have titled him far more formally, "Mr. Kipling."

"Son of a swine!" he bellowed at Tallowgut, but he did not get to lay hands on him, for the big thug cravenly turned tail and fled through the gate. As I disentangled myself from my predicament, I saw Gaiters scramble up from the ground and run away like Tallowgut. Maud chased Ratbag out from behind the hogshead; ducking her blows, he grabbed Braces by the arm—Braces had stood up but looked a bit sick; Ratbag towed him away from the fray, they both vanished out the gate, and I stood with my dagger uselessly poised, for there was no longer anyone for me to bloody it on!

Wiping it on my skirt, therefore, I ran to where Wolcott Balestier lay, and I pulled the rag out of his mouth. I intended to cut the twine that bound his hands and feet—but he looked ghastly! He lay without moving, his open eyes did not focus on me, his skin looked grey. Unable to touch him, I stood there stupidly for a moment, fearing he was dead.

"Balestier!" exclaimed a hoarse, harrowed voice. Mr. Kipling shoved past me to kneel beside his friend, both hands cupping the man's face. "Cotswold!" Ruddy cried. Then he sat on the ground and lifted his friend's limp body into his arms, holding him as if cradling a child.

"He's just barely breathing," he said, his voice taut as a bowstring. "Cotswold!" he begged, hugging his mate, his buddy, to his chest, and a tear ran down his face into his belligerent moustache.

Chapter the Sixteenth

Wolcott Balestier's battered head turned just an iota; he looked up into his friend's wet eyes, and even from where I stood, I could see the hurt man's face brighten ever so slightly.

"Cotswold," Kipling said fiercely yet shakily, "damn you, don't you dare die! Stay with me, you hear, damn it?"

On Cotswold's face appeared a whisper of a smile.

Kipling sat there in tears, hugging his "best friend a man ever had," and I could scarcely believe how deeply I felt for that puffed-up peacock of a man. But, gulping back my feelings, I bent and got busy freeing Cotswold's hands, then his feet, cutting his bonds. Straightening, dagger in hand, I surveyed the scene of the fray; Maud stood in front of a privy with her makeshift cudgel at the ready, to bash Gibface if he moved, no doubt. But he showed no signs of doing so. I sheathed my dagger in the busk of my corset, then turned to Kipling. With far more authority than I had any right to assume, I ordered, "We must get him out of here. Can we carry him if I help you?"

He gave me a startled look, as if he hadn't realised who I was or even that I was there. As if in prayer he appealed to me, "What is the matter with him? Rabies?"

"No. Not yet, and I told you—"

He interrupted. "Then *what*?"

"Starvation, despair, and I think the wound in his leg might have become suppurated. We must get him to a hospital." I stooped to pick up the sick man's legs, but before I could do so, Kipling surged upwards and, without the assistance of his hands, rose to his feet, lifting his friend in his arms as if Cotswold were no heavier than a child. Cradling him, he took a dazed look around him.

"This way," I directed, and led him towards the gate. As we passed the doughty milkmaid, I blurted, "Maud, why are you here?"

"Some eejit asked me for help." She lowered her weapon and turned to follow me.

"That's not what I mean! Here, in London City instead of Shoreditch. Are you not working for Lister anymore?"

"Of course I am!" she grumbled into my ear, walking close behind me. "The milk's me morning job," she complained as she followed Kipling and me around the side of the tenement, "and now I be late wit all my deliveries."

I barely heard her, for just as we reached the street a cab approached, and I ran towards it to commandeer it for Cotswold. A roomy, enclosed four-wheel "growler" such as was seldom to be seen on back streets such as Smutty Lane, it was a godsend, and I intended, I must, I *would* persuade the occupants to relinquish it for Cotswold's sake—

"Enola!" shouted an oddly familiar, imperious voice from above, and my feet stopped me where I was, for I experienced a moment of mystification until the cab halted and a tall man in a city suit leapt down from his seat on the box beside the cabbie.

"Hello, Sherlock," I told him, feeling a great sense of relief that he had arrived at last. But although he stood in front of me, he did not respond to my greeting or even seem to see me anymore. His glance shot past me and he exclaimed, "Kipling! Is that Balestier?"

Mr. Kipling responded in a hoarse, quavering voice, "Yes, it is, and we must get him to a hospital at once!"

I must say my brother and his client made quick work of easing Cotswold into the cab and laying him on the back seat. I watched wistfully for a moment, but as they paid me no attention whatsoever, I turned away as the doors closed, and went to help Maud hang her heavy buckets once more from her yoke and ease the load onto her shoulders.

"Thank you, very much, for what you did," I told her.

"Enjoyed it," she said in her expressionless way. "I 'ave to go."

I stood watching her stride off, and the cab passing her at a fast trot as it left, and it occurred to me that I, also, should be on my way before Gibface pried himself out of the privy. First, however, I crossed Smutty Lane (dodging pedestrians and conveyances of every description, as usual) to the tenement where I had previously found haven.

I had not yet touched the front door when it flew open, and the three shock-headed brothers crowded it like baby birds in a nest, their mouths all wide open at once, crowing at me.

"Lydy, didjer trounce them hooligans, truly?"

"The man yer brought out, is he hurt bad?"

"Miss, I'm no coward, please, ma'am, but I 'ad to leave." This was the oldest, with his stringbean arms wrapped around his younger brothers as he spoke. "I've these two I must look out fer."

"These two" continued to squeal questions, but I paid them no heed, intent on Stringbean, beginning to understand. "Have you no father or mother?" I asked.

"No, ma'am, they both sickened and died. Now it's just us three."

"I see. Then I must thank you even more greatly for your help." I paid them extravagantly, then left their doorstep and walked away—or plodded, rather, for suddenly all strength had left me. It was over, Wolcott

Balestier found and cared for, the fight won, my self-imposed task done, and I had not slept in too long, I felt and looked a wreck, my hair dragging and tangled, my clothing torn and bloodstained, folk staring at me as I stumbled along. Leaving Smutty Lane behind at last, I found myself walking, or trying to walk, beside a more frequented thoroughfare, with carriages and cabs driving past me. But I did not even attempt to hail myself a hansom as I kept unsteadily onward, for I knew no sensible cabbie would accept as a fare any person who looked as drunk and disheveled as I did. I intended—although very vaguely indeed, for my mind seemed to be as weary and draggle-tailed as my body—I thought I would find a station for the Underground, then take a train to . . . somewhere. . . .

Eyes on the pavement in front of my shambling feet, hazily trying to think where I was going, I completely failed to notice a cab making a sudden stop at the kerb ahead of me, until a lady leapt out of it and called in a sweet alto voice, "Miss Holmes!"

Stopping, I raised my head to see who it was: Caroline Balestier, a vision in violet silk, running towards me.

"What has happened to you! Who has done this?

You're bruised, and all bloody!" she cried in her lovely American accent as she reached me, clasping me by the shoulders as if I might fall. Indeed, although I was taller than her, somehow she was looking at the top of my head, for she said in utter shock, "You're wounded!"

"Cotswold is found," I mumbled.

"What!"

I strove to raise my head, face her, and speak more clearly. "Sherlock and Ruddy took Cotswold to the hospital."

She gasped and looked as if she might topple, but she rallied quickly, turning to order in a military tone, "Cabbie, come here! Fetch my shawl!" And a gorgeous mauve shawl it was, I noticed as the cab-driver brought it, or perhaps it was two shawls, or four, or perhaps my eyes would no longer focus. Caroline wrapped the shawl around me. I tried to tell her I would ruin it with dirt, grime, and blood, but my powers of speech did not seem to be working very well, either. I seemed to hear Miss Balestier telling the man to help her get me into the cab, but once they had done that, I closed my eyes and was only vaguely aware of a jouncy sensation, the cab rumbling over cobbles.

I roused somewhat when we reached our destination, the house on Maiden Lane—Miss Balestier had taken me to her home! She and the cab-driver helped me up the front steps, and the parlour-maid flung open the door before we reached it, crying, "Miss Balestier, there's been a message about Mr. Balestier! He's alive, and they've taken him to Saint Thomas's Hospital!"

"I must go right now," said Miss Balestier, greatly perturbed; I could hear how wrought she was, "and you, Sadie, must take the greatest care of our friend—" Quite suddenly she shook me, although not hard, and demanded, face to my dumbfounded face, "For mercy's sake, Miss Holmes, what *is* your first name?"

"Enola," I mumbled.

"Sadie!" Caroline Balestier bespoke the parlour-maid in martial tones. "You are to take the greatest care of Enola, for she is precious to me. Understood?" This was a command rather than question. Carrie thrust me into the servant's arms, then off to the hospital she flew.

And despite my dubious history with Sadie the parlour-maid, care for me she did, taking me in charge as if I were a child, she and the cook and the maid-of-all-help. Putting some cushions on a kitchen chair, they sat me there, and Sadie whisked my clothes off of me and examined me whilst the cook heated water and somebody brought me a nightgown—I am not very clear about any of this. I remember Sadie washing the blood off my head with warm water, tsking over the wound, and doctoring it with something that stung. Someone else then sorted out my tangled hair, someone else applied a washcloth to the messiest parts of me, and somehow they all gathered that I badly needed to be fed, for beef tea and toast appeared before me, along with a dainty glass of water and one of red wine! I am sure I devoured everything, but I admit I remember chiefly the sweetness of the wine, and shortly thereafter, the softness of a bed, the warmth of hot water bottles at my feet, and a nice snuggly sort of feeling. I am sure I was asleep within moments.

. . .

I must have slept throughout what was left of that day and the night that followed, for I was awakened by a maid who brought me a breakfast tray. Breakfast in bed! This was pampering such as I had never in my life previously enjoyed! The breakfast, a bowl of porridge topped with strawberries, appeared quite luscious, and so it was, and I was just savouring the last bite when someone knocked, then entered the bedroom without waiting for an answer.

It was Sherlock, looking a bit the worse for wear, unshaven, with some smudges on his crisp white shirt cuffs.

At the sight of him I sat bolt upright, knocking over the tray. "How is Cotswold?" I demanded.

Sherlock responded with an annoying sort of bow. "Good morning."

"How *is* he?"

"Miss Balestier was good enough to tell me where I might find you."

"Sherlock!" I grew louder by the moment.

"She mentioned that she was looking for Agatha Bellwether when she happened upon you."

"How very quaint. Sherlock, I asked you—"

Taking no notice, he gazed around him. "And I believe this is Caroline Balestier's very own bedroom."

"Sherlock, *please!*"

He finally turned to me and gave me one of his faint smiles. "Mr. Balestier lived through the night and appears quite likely to live through the day also, and the next night, and so forth." Sherlock sat down on a dainty French round-backed chair. "And you seem to be quite yourself again, Enola?"

I felt myself blush. "It was just that I had been up all night," I said, "with no food or drink."

"And it was just that you had been exhausted whilst battling for a man's life," added Sherlock, straight-faced.

As was often the case when I was with him, I could find no reply to make.

"In any event, it seems affairs are improving," Sherlock continued, "and I think it is likely Miss Balestier might desire the use of her bed for herself soon, so I have come to offer you a ride back to the Professional Women's Club."

"In this?" I looked down at my borrowed nightgown, which, I now noticed, was decorated with pink ribbons and lace, very likely belonging to Miss Balestier as much as the bed did.

"Of course not," Sherlock said. "Take it off and wrap yourself in a blanket."

I sputtered in horror, but at that moment the day-maid entered, carrying my clothes on high before her: the clothes I had all but ruined yesterday, now clean, dry, and folded to perfection. Even my boots, topping the pile, looked good as new.

"My goodness!" I gasped.

"Ran a wash-line over the stove to dry them all night, Cook did," said the maid, smiling at me as she put the clothes on Miss Caroline's dresser, then departed.

No sooner was she out the door than Sherlock said in that peremptory way of his, "Enola, I do not have time to stay any longer. Take a cab home." He planted funds for the fare on top of my pile of clothes. "And kindly, without fail, present yourself for tea at Baker Street this afternoon. *Au revoir.*" He strode out.

I was left momentarily speechless. But then, quite softly so no one would hear, I said a few naughty things, and then I got out of bed.

Doing this, I discovered that my personage was harbouring a good many aches and pains. I had to ring for rubbing alcohol, which I applied liberally to all the affected areas, never mind the smell. Dressing my sore self was a bit more difficult than usual, but I managed, then sallied forth from the bedroom to render sincere, indeed heartfelt, thanks to Cook, Sadie the parlour-maid, all the women who had taken "the greatest care of me," to discover that, as a final favour, they had already secured a cab for me!

. . .

"Great jumping Jehoshaphat, Enola, what happened to you?" exclaimed the first friend I encountered when I entered the Professional Women's Club.

Others crowded around. "You have been gone two nights," cried my favourite phrenologist. "We were worried about you!"

"You're all bruised," chimed in another, "and I smell rubbing alcohol, and is that a *wound* on your head?" This they all could see, for my hair hung down, and I had no hat.

"Wherever have you been, Enola?" demanded yet another of my friends.

"Patience, patience," I told them, making my way to the sitting room, as the parlour seemed too formal for my disheveled state of being. Settling myself in a comfortable wing chair, I waited until the others had gathered—so many that there was standing room only—and then I started, "Well, if you really *must* know, I rode a cow past Covent Garden, but it bucked me off."

I heard titters as they began to realise I was not at all serious, but telling them a silly story just to amuse them.

"And then I spent some time peddling tinware on the streets, until I found a more rewarding pastime cleaning up after the dogs in a very exclusive kennel."

Titters gave way to hearty laughter.

"After which I became embroiled in a disagreement with five numbskulls of ill repute," I told them, "but I emerged mostly unscathed, and now, if you will excuse me, I really must go put my hair up." Still laughing as I arose, they clapped their hands, and I bowed to left and right before I exited the room.

"What a jolly fellow she is, truly!" I heard some chuckling colleague say as I departed.

"But I wonder where she has been, really?" said another.

They would never know.

• • •

Upstairs, in my room, I sighed deeply for some reason I could not quite name, then rid myself of boots and clothing, put on my softest dressing-gown and slippers, and rang for a maid to help deal with my hair. Also, I used my speaking-tube to the kitchen to ask for a plate of cheese and pickle sandwiches to be sent up, for it appeared my toilette would take some time.

And so it did, for the maid clucked over my wounded scalp, and we conferred about how best to arrange it so that I could wear a hat to hide the scab Gibface had given me.

I had devoured the sandwiches before we finished, the maid having arranged my deplorable hair in a sort of horseshoe-shaped sausage circumventing the damage atop my head. I thanked her profusely as she left, and also I asked her to send a boy to take a message to Harold.

Then I opened my wardrobe and stood befuddled in front of it for some time: what to put on for today's "without fail" tea? Usually (or actually, not very usually) when I went for tea at my famous brother's flat, I dressed to my utmost, getting myself all done up in full caparison, in order to amuse and annoy him. But this felt like a more serious occasion. So: not my new summer frock, all cerulean ruffles, nor any of my other colourful dresses, either. Actually, Sherlock might not care what I wore, but I myself cared, confound it. Scowling, I yanked garment after garment from my overfull wardrobe, and achieved success at last, choosing an outfit newly fashionable among progressive women: a narrow skirt and "shirt waist" blouse complete with puff tie, along with a plain, frankly mannish hat. In this modern attire I felt as if no one could perceive me as either frivolous or strait-waisted. I wanted to be seen, quite simply, as myself.

Chapter the Seventeenth

After Harold dropped me off at 221 Baker Street and Mrs. Hudson had let me in, I stood outside the door of Sherlock's flat for a hesitant moment before I knocked. My brother's peremptory invitation to tea had unnerved me.

"Come in!" called the familiar voice of the inhabitant.

I opened the door and saw Sherlock lounging in his usual chair and smoking his usual pipe, but not in his usual mouse-coloured dressing-gown. He was attired quite formally, as if he were going out for dinner.

"Any news of Wolcott Balestier?" I demanded.

My brother raised his expressive eyebrows. "And good afternoon to you, too, my dear sis—"

"How is he *doing*?" I interrupted quite forcibly.

A slightly querulous voice, not Sherlock's, replied, "Cotswold is doing well and is going to be all right, all benevolent gods be praised."

Flabbergasted, I pushed the door farther open and saw Rudyard Kipling, like my brother in formal dress, rise from his chair with a slight inclination of his head towards me, as if a lady was entering the room.

So taken aback that I found myself speechless, I walked in. "Miss Holmes," Kipling said with utmost courtesy, "it is a great pleasure to see you again, but where is Oscar Wilde today?"

Sherlock gave him a puzzled look, as well he might.

But mischief in Kipling's eyes immediately roused me to respond, "I did not know that you and your peculiar proclivities were going to be here today."

"Ah. Quite so. But both your brother and I most anxiously wish to know how you managed to find my friend Balestier."

"Sit down, Enola," directed my brother.

In order to do so, I needed to clear a space on his

camel-back sofa, and I gave him a dark look as I did so. "You invited me for *tea*. And where is Miss Balestier, as we seem to be having a social gathering?"

"At her brother's bedside, of course, or else at home resting. Do please sit."

Rolling my eyes heavenwards, I did so.

In propitiating tones, at least for him, Sherlock said to me, "Now, I promise I will feed you immediately after you tell me how you came to be dagger fighting, yesterday morning, against my fellow members of the Mark of the Ichneumon."

Now Kipling looked puzzled.

I sighed, and told Sherlock, "I followed Mary Erasmus."

"Please indulge us with a bit more specificity, if you would be so good."

Knowing that any further eye-rolling was useless, I leaned back on the sofa, settling in to relate what had happened on Thursday evening, a mere two days ago. I explained my reasons for wanting to locate Mary Erasmus, and described how I did so, and how I found her, and how—at this point I took care to use my most matter-of-fact tone of voice—I was captured.

Sherlock tsked. "You have no proper knowledge of how to shadow people, Enola," he said.

I ignored this remark. "They took me up to the very top of the tenement and into an exceedingly squalid room, where I saw Wolcott Balestier, bound hand and foot, leaning against a wall and looking not well at all."

Kipling whispered something heartfelt and unrepeatable.

I went on. "Mary Erasmus cursed me thoroughly and then left me in the hands of her scruffy henchmen, ordering them to 'take care of me.'"

Ruddy demanded, "Who the dickens is Mary Erasmus?"

"Their leader. A remarkably duplicitous and treacherous young woman," I said. "An ichneumon of a woman. She is both a rescuing mongoose and a poisoning, parasitic wasp."

"In other words, you know very little about her," summarised Sherlock, perhaps a bit unfairly. "We must find her and have the law deal with her."

Without saying so, I thought this was unlikely to happen. She was clever, and what did we know of her? That her father was a whitesmith?

And, months later, as I write this account, it would seem I was correct. The police and my brother and I combined have found no trace of her.

Sherlock continued, "But Enola, how did you escape?"

"I bespoke Cotswold in verbiage of Shakespearean provenance, deeming that the miscreants might not divine it—"

Both of my listeners were staring at me as if I had gone quite mad, so I told them the rest in plain English: how Cotswold had roused enough to respond "like the perspicacious yet charming gentleman he is, Mr. Kipling."

Ruddy's face showed such warm emotion that he seemed unable to speak.

I continued. "In order to encourage him and offer him hope, I informed him about the amazing possibilities of Lister's inoculation. By the way, have you contacted Lister?"

Kipling swallowed and spoke. "Yes! Yes, what a splendid chap. He is eager to start treatment as soon as Cotswold is a bit stronger."

"Enola," Sherlock iterated, "how did you escape?"

282

I told them. Sherlock was horrified by the unsanitary method I used, but Ruddy appeared to be trying not to grin.

"But Balestier was not physically able to flee with you," said Sherlock.

All amusement disappeared from Kipling's face at once.

"He managed to block the door for a while," I said, "and I am afraid they treated him quite roughly, afterwards."

"May cruel Diti get her claws on them," said Kipling in a taut voice.

"I quite agree," I said, "but I would not have reached the street if it were not for Cotswold's delaying the pursuit."

Sherlock leaned forward with the intent look of a hunting hawk on his angular face. "Enola, who were these men, exactly?"

Peeling off my gloves and laying them aside, I reached for paper and pencil. Sketching Gibface and the others in detail, I went on with my narrative as I worked, telling how I had hidden atop the pediment (Ruddy gave a low whistle), and then I had taken refuge in the tenement across the street, making the startled acquaintance of three barefoot brothers. "I sent the oldest to watch the enemy stronghold from the back, and the younger two with messages—"

"We know," said my brother in his driest tone. "I was shaving." He gave Kipling an interrogatory look.

"I had just finished dressing," said Ruddy, "and it's a good thing, for I would have gone in my smalls."

"I've seldom seen a more compelling missive," agreed Sherlock. "What were you doing meanwhile, Enola?"

"Sitting on the floor by the window across the street, keeping watch surreptitiously, and stuffing my mouth with lemon drops." As I spoke, I continued drawing my rogues' gallery. I had completed faces of all five men, and was now sketching Tallowgut's unattractive physique. "I had already seen Gibface and Gaiters return in very ill humour from having failed to chase me down, which was quite all right with me, but when I caught sight of Ratbag and Braces approaching—"

Kipling, looking befuddled, opened his mouth to question, but Sherlock anticipated him. "She assigned names to the thugs in question. It's sublimely typical of her."

I am afraid I rather glared at him.

"Ratbag and Braces arrived to be reinforcements?" he prompted me.

"Yes, and when I saw them go in, I became quite alarmed, for I knew it meant trouble." My drawings completed, I shoved them aside and gestured rather wildly with my hands. "I ran out into the street with some vague idea of dashing to Cotswold's rescue, and blundered into Maud. The milkmaid," I added by way of explanation. "Maud really is her name." And then, seeing from their blank faces that more and further explanation was necessary, "I met her at Lister's kennels, I mean, um, laboratory, in Shoreditch."

"Never mind, Enola," said Sherlock gently enough. "Go on."

"So then Stringbean came running—"

"Stringbean?" Sherlock murmured.

"The oldest boy! He came running to tell me the Mark of thick-new-man was taking Cotswold out the back, and I ran to do my best to discourage them with my dagger, but I would have been flattened if it were not for Maud."

And I would have been killed if it were not for Ruddy, I was thinking, but how to thank him?

As if he had read my mind and wanted to head me off, Kipling turned to my brother and said, "When I arrived, your sister had bloodied them extensively with her darting blade, and the milkmaid was clouting their heads with her yoke, and soon every mother's son of them ran away."

"We must have the police round them up," said Sherlock, making a long arm from his chair to my sofa, gathering up my drawings of Gibface et cetera, and looking through them with an approving nod. "Enola, at your earliest convenience, you must go to Scotland Yard and make a report on everything you have told us, with emphasis upon Mary Erasmus. She needs to be arrested for conspiracy to have you captured and held against your will."

Listening to him ordering me about irritated me, and I responded bluntly, "At your earliest convenience, I should like my tea."

It irritated me even more that Sherlock then seemed amused. Gravely bowing his head to me, he said entirely too humbly, "I shall see to it." He then got up, went out the door, stood at the top of the stairs, and bellowed, "Mrs. Hudson!" Then, as Mrs. Hudson did not immediately respond, he clattered downstairs to get her.

"Miss Holmes," said Mr. Kipling.

I gave him my startled attention, especially as he got up from his armchair and crossed the room to sit on the sofa beside me. He looked very serious in a strange but not frightening way. He faced me eye to eye and said, "That knuckleheaded man who called you names when he first met you last week, he was a great gumptious buffoon and a rollicking dunderhead. He did not realise your caliber, Miss Holmes." Ruddy gave me a sort of seated bow, then reached towards me. "Might I kiss your hand?"

Already I had drawn back. "And prickle my maidenly skin with that pusillanimous moustache of yours? No, thank you."

Oddly, my refusal seemed to please him. Although one could not tell for sure because of the aforementioned moustache, he almost seemed to smile. "Well, then, I shall salute you like the gallant soldier you are, Miss Enola Holmes," he said.

And he did so.

Epilogue

"Did it hurt dreadfully?" Caroline Balestier asked her brother, returning to his bedroom after showing Dr. Lister out with many thanks and the fullest ceremony of obligation. Wolcott, home from the hospital but still on the mend, had just received his first inoculation, concocted from a rabid rabbit's spinal cord that had been dried for fifteen days. The next inoculation, tomorrow, would be from a spinal cord that had been dried for fourteen days, and then thirteen, and so on until Dr. Lister could inoculate no more, or the spinal cord would have been still inside the living, raving, rabid rabbit.

Lying in bed amidst a number of hot water bottles, Wolcott replied with a brave, puckish smile, "No, it doesn't hurt a bit," but then apparently changed his mind. "That was a dreadful fib, Carrie. It hurt atrociously, and still does, and will continue to do so. Would you care to guess where, exactly, on my anatomy he injected it?"

"Heavens! No, dear."

"I shall tell you just the same: in the skin of my abdomen, of all places. And he will be back tomorrow to do it again, and the next day, and the day after that—" Wolcott sat up in bed, alarmingly round-eyed. "—for two ghastly weeks, until he is certain that I am well and truly perforated against rabies."

Trying not to frown, Caroline undertook her duty as an upper-class woman to guide the morals and behaviour of her family. "Now, Wolcott—"

But her brother interrupted. "Oh, hush, Carrie." Leaning back against his pillows, he took one of the hot water bottles, hugged it against the part of him that was in pain, and gave her an impish grin. "I know I am being saved from a horrible death, and I know I should be grateful, and indeed I am, truly. Dr. Lister is perfectly splendid, and so are you, and Ruddy."

Caroline felt her face soften and glow, not because of her brother's praise, but because of his mention of Ruddy, who had been visiting daily. Ostensibly Ruddy came to see Wolcott, of course, but it was she, Carrie, who always met him at the door. She brightened at the thought.

"You are both simply topping," Wolcott was saying, "but we must not forget—what did you tell me was her name? That tremendously interesting and daring young woman who carries a dagger in her bosom?"

Caroline's dark eyes widened and her firm jaw almost appeared to drop. *"A dagger in her bosom?"*

"Yes, quite! She cut my bonds with it."

"Eccentric as she is, still, I would not think that Enola Holmes—"

"Enola Holmes! Yes, that's her name. Is she—"

But a polite knock on his bedroom door interrupted Wolcott, and he heard Sadie, the parlour-maid, announce, "Enola Holmes to visit Mr. Balestier, if it is not too inconvenient."

Wolcott glanced at his sister to find that her pleased expression mirrored his. He nodded.

"By all means, send her in!" Carrie called, and both

she and Wolcott smiled broadly as the tall, angular young woman entered the room, carrying a bouquet of daffodils and daisies. She wore a white hat with ribbons and a quite lovely frock of a primrose shade printed all over with tiny mauve flowers, with white lace trimming. Oddly, awkward and gawky as Enola was, in the dainty dress she looked quite sweet.

Caroline stood to greet her, but before she could say a word, Wolcott sang from his bed, "Grateful salutations and most humble accolades to thee, O lion-hearted warrior maiden!"

Setting the flowers on the dresser, Enola blinked at him, wordless, almost shy.

"But dost thou not bear thy dauntless dagger this day?" he added, seeing no bulbous red brooch on her bosom.

Her look turned from shy to sparkling, and in a lilting voice she said, "Verily, O sorely afflicted soul, for thy sake and the succor of all in thrall, ever and always—" She touched a large opal adorning the front of her frock, then gripped it to draw her dagger with a flourish.

Caroline gasped and stepped back.

But Enola sedately sheathed her dagger in the busk

of her corset. "My apologies," she said to Carrie. "I was caught up in the romance of the moment." And to Wolcott she said in a thoroughly normal tone, "Necessarily, for fashion's sake I possess more than one."

"Forsooth," he gasped, trying not to laugh, because laughing hurt him. Meanwhile, Caroline recovered and stepped forwards, hand outstretched in greeting. "How very good to see you again," she said cordially. "Won't you have a seat?" She indicated the straight-back wooden chair she had been occupying, it being the only one in the small bedroom.

"No, thank you. I cannot stay long." Caroline was relieved to note that Enola did, after all, have some manners.

Wait. Something about Enola's tone of voice, so polite for a change, so socially correct, took Caroline back to the truly first time she had seen that angular woman, that aquiline profile. Suddenly standing on tiptoe, she pointed at Enola like a child. "You were there!" she cried. "That very first night, on the corner where I was showing Wolcott's portrait, you inquired!"

Enola gave her a pleased look, mildly surprised. "You have an extraordinarily good memory for faces."

Lowering her heels and her hand, Caroline felt herself blush at her own impropriety. All the more so when Enola grinned impishly at her and said, "It's my nose, isn't it?"

It was. But Caroline babbled, "No, really . . ."

Wolcott saved his sister. "Enola Holmes." Even though he lay flat on his back in his bed, his formal tone demanded attention. "I have not yet thanked you for saving my life." He tried to sit up. "I owe you my eternal gratitude."

It was Enola's turn to blush. "It was really Ruddy who saved you."

"He would disagree. You know he thinks the world of you."

Enola smiled fit to light up the room. "When we first met, he called me an ostrich biddy with the mouth of a muleteer."

"Aha! He liked you already!"

"As did I, the very first time we met," said Caroline, who had recovered her social balance.

"Claptrap and balderdash, both of you," said Enola tenderly. "This sort of nonsense is why I am delighted to know you. But now I really must be going. One must not weary the invalid." She shook hands with Wolcott, kissed Caroline on the cheek, and strode out with a swirl of her pretty skirt.

Caroline sank back into her chair, feeling oddly exhausted.

Her brother asked, "What was all that about her being there 'the very first night'?"

Carrie turned to face him. "When I first knew you were missing, I stood outdoors like a madwoman showing your picture, and Enola 'just happened by.'" She put a wry twist on the last three words.

"You mean that already, within twenty-four hours, she was on my trail?"

"Yes, but, you see, Ruddy had something to do with that."

"He told me he called her names."

"Yes!" And at the thought of Ruddy calling names, his habitual distrust of women, his cleft chin advanced in a bristling frown, Carrie Balestier surprised herself by laughing joyously, for she knew herself to be the West to his East.

Author's Note

Since my childhood, the works of Rudyard Kipling have entranced me. As a writer, I owe a great deal to the influence of his poetic prose, for the sake of which I excused him for being a bit of a misogynist, like many men of his era. It is historical fact that he lived in London during 1890, he was the toast of the town, and he was writing his first novel, *The Light That Failed*. It is historical fact, also, that during this period Kipling formed an extraordinarily close friendship with Wolcott Balestier, an American writer/editor/publisher who was visiting London along with his sister, Caroline. And it is historical fact that, in due time, Caroline Balestier married Kipling, and remained married to him for the next forty-four years, despite his famously moody nature.

Because I admire Kipling's writing so much but must tolerate his misogyny to do so, I could not resist fictitiously confronting him with my Suffragist brainchild Enola Holmes. My characterizations of Kipling, Wolcott Balestier, and Carrie Balestier are based on research, yet ultimately imaginary. Similarly, I researched Joseph Lister, an important historical personage, but my interpretation of his personality is my own creation. Mary Erasmus and the Mark of the Ichneumon are totally fictitious. Likewise, it is totally fiction that Wolcott Balestier was bitten by a rabid dog, then abducted; none of this ever actually happened. And of course, one must remind oneself that Enola Holmes, like her brother Sherlock Holmes, is a fictitious character.

I do hope you enjoyed this novel, gentle reader.